MW01136130

This is a work of fiction.
either a product of the a
Any resemblance to actu.
whether living or dead, is entirely coincidental.

THE BOOK CLUB MURDERS

Previous books written by this author include:
"Trust Me Now"
"Cassandra's Moon"

Contact the author at ollmanjeff@gmail.com or go to his blog
site at jeffreyollman.blogspot.com

ISBN-13: 978-1496150486
ISBN-10 1496150481

Introduction

The inspiration for this novel began when my wife hosted a book club meeting a couple of years ago. The members had gathered to discuss my first book, Trust Me Now. I was the "guest" author in my own home. The ladies were very kind to me and brought up no inconsistencies or examples of poor writing on my part and acted like they had enjoyed the book. All in all, it made me feel quite good. At the conclusion of the meeting, one of the ladies told me, in jest, I think, that I should write a book about them. The idea immediately struck me and I filed it away. A month later, I was hard at work on, The Book Club Murders. Should you choose to continue reading, the result awaits you. I hope you enjoy.

Chapter 1

Rose Creek, Minnesota

January 6, 2014

She watched and waited, shielded from view by the protective shadows of trees across the street. It was 10:08 p.m. The porch light had flicked on and the door had opened. Laughter permeated the air as women filtered out of the house, saying their goodbyes and then getting into their cars and driving away.

Laura Walters was the last to leave. She stood clearly illuminated in the porch light as she shared laughs and final words with the host of the monthly book club meeting. Laura said her last goodbye as she turned, exited the porch, and began the four block walk to her home, a neatly kept two story colonial on the northern side of County Road 4.

The four glasses of wine she had drunk during the "meeting" seemed to warm her innards, although she still pulled the collar tighter against her exposed neck. She wore no hat as she braved the winter chill and negotiated the icy sidewalk guiding her to her house, slipping and sliding a little as she proceeded. A wordless, ephemeral melody flowed from her lips, guaranteeing that she would pay little attention to her surroundings. She had no idea that she was being followed.

Nightstick in hand, the stalker inched closer to her target until she was only a few steps behind.

The night was quiet except for Laura's singing and the crunching sound made when their boots mashed chunks of ice on the sidewalk. Both figures stopped when Laura saw the shadow of another figure

3

close to hers. She ceased vocalizing the wordless melody and turned to see the one behind her.

Her eyes brightened, losing the dull sheen of inebriety. "I thought-" Before Laura could finish the sentence the nightstick crashed into her skull several times, sprinkling the sidewalk and snow with spatters of her blood.

Breathing heavily, the stalker removed a glove and felt for a pulse in Laura's neck. There was none. "One down," she said to no one and then left.

Claude lay in bed, eyes closed, but nonetheless, awake. His bedroom was exceedingly warm causing him to sweat buckets until his sheets felt saturated. Funny, it was winter and he thought he had turned the heat down to 58 degrees earlier in the evening. He slept best when a chill was in the air and the ceiling fan delivered just enough of a gentle breeze to keep him comfortable.

It wasn't long before he couldn't stand it anymore and he threw the top sheet and light blanket off as his eyes sprang open. Five seconds later, his eyes adjusted to the blackness, revealing her standing near the end of the bed.

"What are you doing here? What time is it?" he frantically asked.

Moving around the corner of the bed, she edged closer. "Does it matter?"

Claude had thought he would never see her again. Fear seeped into his brain as he wondered how she had entered his apartment. And the heat, the damn heat and sweat were driving him insane. He was literally swimming in his own sweat soaked sheets and trembling as he watched her come closer.

"I thought we needed some time together," she said while removing her clothes and nestling close to his body, making the sweaty heat even more unbearable.

"I, I can't. It's too hot in here. Let me turn down the heat," he pleaded.

"You know I like it this way. Stay in bed." He felt her hand on his thigh. She then began.

He felt himself involuntarily harden as her hand grasped him.

"No, no, no," he said, barely audible even to himself.

She continued as he gulped for air, sweating, dreading every second, almost not noticing she had mounted him and had begun rhythmically rocking. Her hair brushed over and back across her face as she moved, but he didn't see. His eyes had closed when she had begun; he had not wanted to look at her. Soon, however, their bodies were cooperating, moving in tandem to the rhythm dictated by her.

When he climaxed, she quickened her pace until she screamed and collapsed upon his chest.

Tears that he never saw rolled from her eyes, mixing with their sweat.

They lay like that for several minutes until, exhausted, she slid off him and rolled to the other side of the bed. Claude gathered himself, noticed that the digital clock read 11:45p.m., and slunk toward the bathroom, first stopping at the thermostat to turn the heat down. He closed the door before turning on the light to avoid waking her; he didn't want that. He turned the shower on and kept the water cool. He stood, letting the cold water pelt his face, hair and body, turning so his back and buttocks could feel the cleansing, cooling spray. Grasping the bar of soap, he scrubbed himself until his skin was red and tender to the touch.

Sheriff Cooper Lewis sat in his relaxed style, leaned back with his feet up on his desk in Spirit Grove. He cradled a hot, bitter, cup of coffee in his hands and just sat, relaxing while he waited for Deputy Lisa Dolcheski to arrive for work. At 8:04 a.m., the door swung open and Lisa popped in.

Lewis caught her eye and pointed toward the clock hanging above Lisa's head. "You're late," he said amiably with a little smirk.

"I'm sorry, Cooper. I got caught up with a marathon session of Star Trek episodes and stayed up too late."

"Never knew you were a Trekkie, Lisa."

"Oh yeah, big time. I love that show. Anytime I see that it's going to be on I try to make sure I watch it."

"You should just get a DVR, record it, and watch it anytime you want. Then, maybe you won't stay up so late and be late for work the next morning." He smiled when he said the last part.

"It won't happen again, Cooper." She had said it while making clear she knew he was only joking.

She poured herself a cup of coffee, took a sip and grimaced. "I'll make us a new batch," she said as she retained her grip on the pot and poured it out in the sink. "So, anything new this early in the morning?"

"Nothing that I know of. Looks like a nice, relaxing day at the office," he said as he leaned back even further in his swivel chair, nearly tipping over.

Lisa fiddled with measuring the coffee into the filter as Lewis studied her. She was tall, although several inches shorter than his six foot nine frame. Tall, athletic, even pretty when she allowed herself to be. He often wondered, where were all of the eligible men? Here was a great catch and no suitors. He knew that if he weren't taken and old enough to be her father, he'd be asking her out in a hurry.

"Cooper, I've got the Rose Creek police department on line two," barked Pat Schminsky, dispatcher and secretary for the last five years.

"Probably Derrick Hansen wanting me to go fishing on Saturday," Lewis said, smiling and nodding knowingly at Lisa. He picked up the phone and tried to start bantering, but was cut off by Hansen. Lewis's face drooped and he lost the happy tone in his voice. He continued listening, occasionally asking a question. He was stone faced when he hung up and just sat and stared out the window.

The coffee maker gave off its three beeps, indicating it was done, and Lisa poured two cups. She quietly walked to where Cooper Lewis sat and held one out. When Cooper didn't reach for it, her hand lingered in place for a few seconds before placing the cup on a piece of cardboard that served as a coaster.

After stepping back a few feet, she asked, "What's wrong, Cooper?"

His stare continued straight ahead when he answered, "A woman was found dead on the sidewalk a few blocks from Highway 56 in Rose Creek." He paused a while, looked up at Lisa, then continued, "Hansen says she was murdered."

Pat Schminski, earphones plugged in, continued typing, oblivious to the conversation. Lisa looked visibly shaken, but recovered quickly. "We haven't had a murder for quite a while around here." She cautiously asked, "Who was it?"

Lewis picked up his coffee and took a sip, "Laura Walters," he said.

Except for the pounding on the keyboard, silence ruled for several seconds until Lisa spoke again, "I know, uh... knew Laura." Her hands were fiddling with the cup and her eyes were cast down to the floor.

"I know, Lisa. I knew her too. Not very well, but enough to say that she was a fun, joyful person." There was another painful pause before Cooper said that Derrick Hansen had asked if he could assist with the investigation.

"When do we start?" Lisa asked.

"Now. I'm heading over there right away. So much for a nice, relaxing day, heh?"

"I'll grab my coat and come with you," said Lisa.

Lewis stood up. "No, not this time, Lisa. She was a friend of yours and I'm so sorry, but one of us should stay here." She looked disappointed, but knew that one of them had to remain in town and take care of anything that might come up locally. She nodded her head.

Lewis put a hand on her shoulder and gave a comforting squeeze as he passed her by. Lisa gave him a brief, appreciative smile and then walked to her desk. A neatly stacked pile of yesterday's unfinished paperwork had been placed in a corner.

Pat Schminsky removed her earphones. "If you finish those papers this morning, I'll be able to get at them this afternoon, Lisa." Lisa didn't hear a word.

Chapter 2

At 8 a.m., Carin Loggerton sat up quickly when she heard Laura Walter's name. Her right hand shot to the remote to turn up the TV volume.

She couldn't believe what she was hearing. Laura was dead? Murdered? She had just seen her last night at the book club meeting. Oh my God! Her head shook as her pulse quickened. She strained to hear more details from the newswoman, but it had been only a brief report with a promise of more information to be released on the six o'clock news.

Carin reached for her phone and called Mary Bono, a good friend and member of the book club. The phone rang several times before Mary answered.

Not even saying hello, Carin blurted, "Did you hear the news this morning?"

"Actually, I just got up," Mary said groggily.

"Laura Walters was killed last night, maybe murdered." It didn't sink through Mary's brain yet. "Did you hear me?" Carin repeated the words slowly with more emphasis. "Laura Walters was killed last night."

"Oh my God! What...what happened?"

"It was just on the news, really sketchy with no details. There'll be more on the six o'clock news."

"Have you called anyone else, yet?" Mary asked.

"No, I haven't. Only you." Carin's cell phone beeped twice as she was talking to Mary. "Jennie's on the other line. I'd better talk to her. Bye." She disconnected Mary quickly and answered Jennie's call.

"Did you hear the news this morning?" Jennie asked. "I can't believe it."

"I did. It's just terrible. We just had a great time with her last night. Did you hear they think she might have been murdered?" Carin asked through her tears.

Beth got the call from Carin right before she was going to head to her office. She, along with Damien, was a full-fledged private investigator now, licensed by the State of Minnesota. Damien had also retained his sideline business as a Krav Maga instructor.

Krav Maga was a form of self-defense training that involved brutal attack and counter attack methods to overcome an aggressor in the real world. Beth had been forced to use the Krav Maga methods in the bluff-lands near Lanesboro in a fight for her life against Richard Armtree and Cassandra Ristarn. She had become quite the lethal force in her own right, rivaling Damien in skill, ferociousness, and aptitude.

Carin briefly filled her in. After recovering from the shocking news, Beth answered, "Of course I can meet you guys for lunch at one. The Oak Grill? I'll see you then." Beth hung up the cell phone and placed it on the table, but an instant later she picked it up again and called Damien. He had left their house in Stewartville earlier to meet with Kahler Hotel officials to continue his arrangement for Krav Maga training in a basement room of one of their facilities in Rochester.

They were not married, but had decided to live together for a trial period before making a commitment to marriage. So far, it had been working out quite well. Beth was getting used to a male who needed intensive training putting the toilet seat back down, dribbling on the floor, and leaving a mess on the countertop after making a sandwich. Damien was getting used to the idea of living with someone who appeared to be far more particular than he was in general household etiquette and maintenance. Neither one had ever lived with someone of the opposite sex before, so conflicts were bound to happen, and did.

She got a hold of Damien, told him of the death of Laura Walters, the luncheon with the rest of the Austin book club members, and that she would check in at the office on any possible clients before leaving for lunch.

Business had not exactly been booming since they started their practice a month and a half earlier. Only two relatively minor cases had been handled by them: a missing daughter who turned out to be sleeping over at her boyfriend's house, and a dispute between a dog owner and his neighbor who hired their fledgling firm to find a way to quiet the barking dog at night. There had been no high profile, well paying jobs.

They had cleared up the barking dog problem by negotiating with the dog owner, something the neighbor had tried, but in an extremely emotional manner that resulted only in increased anger and frustration. The owner of the dog, an elderly lady, had eventually seen the light (after sharing two glasses of wine and a relaxing discussion with Beth). The two had hit it off immediately and soon had developed not only a plan to quiet the barking dog, but also a continuing friendship that Beth hoped would last for the remainder of the delightful, old lady's lifetime.

She and Damien were hopeful things would pick up as their name firm's name Reddy and Associate, as well as their reputation for success became better known.

Checking in at the office involved walking through the connecting doorway to the former living room which had been walled off from the rest of the house. They had also added an outside entrance to give the building a more professional appearance; their limited budget had not allowed for an office in downtown Stewartville or Rochester.

She checked email and phone messages but finding nothing involving work, she went out the front door to check the snail mail. Nothing there as well, so she decided the best thing to do would be to just hang out until she had to leave for her luncheon date. Never a very patient person, she soon tired of simply doing nothing and drifted into thinking about last night at the book club meeting in Rose Creek.

It had been a great time discussing their book The Lighthouse Road, while also enjoying wine, snacks, and some of the latest area gossip. Of course, everyone got involved in the gossip. After all, who doesn't enjoy the latest rumors regarding the local elites?

Beth thought of Laura and how much she had liked her. She had been a fifty-six year old woman with a husband, three grown kids, and a great sense of humor. Who would ever want to kill someone like that? The more she thought about it, the more the question increasingly bothered her. A random act? A calculated murder? An accident? Nothing made any sense to her. She was sure they would find out more details when they met at the Oak Grill. At least one book club member, Nona Daphne, had connections to the local law enforcement agencies and would be able to share some of her information.

Carin hung up after her last call. It had been to Brenda Edinsel, a teacher working at Neveln, an elementary school on Austin's northeast side. She only had a half hour for lunch, but said she could make it by 1p.m. and meet for the first ten minutes. All of the other book club members, either retired or possessing flexible schedules, had said they could also meet.

That day the Oak Grill, uncharacteristically, had been pretty slow until the women from the book club started showing up. Carin, who was the first to arrive, was able to corral two large round tables in a corner of the restaurant. The rest of the group soon showed up and took their seats quietly as they arrived. The mood was somber; no one was extremely talkative beyond subdued greetings and niceties.

The club consisted of Carin Loggerton, Mary Bono, Jennie Landro, Brenda Edinsel, Penny Schied, Darya Watson, Katy Bar, Celia Orth, Kassidy Medicreek, Cadence Pieson, Galena Mendez, Beth Reddy, Tanya Jinle and Nona Daphne, the one with law enforcement connections.

Carin began, "We'd better get started because Brenda has only a few minutes before she has to get back to work. First, thanks everyone for coming today. It's just a terrible reason to get together, but a few of us thought we could all just help support each other and maybe learn a few facts from Nona about what happened. Nona, if you could let us know what you found out that would be great."

Nona Daphne's cousin was a police officer in town who, when pressed by Nona, would share information with her before it went to the news outlets. She was always sworn to secrecy until the information reached the public, which in this case, would be today at a 2 p.m. press conference.

Nona began haltingly, recounting the details told to her. "She was hit with some kind of blunt object as she walked home, they don't know what, but evidently she was facing her attacker when it happened." Nona stopped and took a deep breath before continuing. She had shared information before with the book club members, but it was always about someone they had not known. This was difficult for her and the rest of the club because Laura had been their friend.

The others gave her time and understanding as they waited for her to continue. "The police think she might have known who killed her because there were no defensive wounds. It didn't appear that she tried to defend herself," she said in a barely audible voice. "That's really all they know right now." She folded her hands on her lap and stared at the table.

An uncomfortable silence engulfed the group as everyone tried to digest the fact that Laura was really dead. Not just dead, but murdered. And, more disturbingly, it may have been done by someone she knew.

Mary Bono finally broke the silence.

"I think that we should hire Beth and Damien to investigate this," she said.

Beth objected immediately.

"I don't know if that would be appropriate right now. The police have barely begun the investigation and, to tell you the truth, I wouldn't even know where to begin."

"But you could just kind of do some checking-under the radar, you know. You're a private investigator, have the necessary training, and you have knowledge of at least some of the people Laura knew," Penny said.

"I don't think this is a good idea," Cadence protested. "The police have barely started, and if we get someone poking around it might seem like we're meddling in the investigation."

The group began warming to the discussion, momentarily forgetting their sadness. Darya and Celia suggested hiring Beth and Damien. The rest, except for Cadence and Katy voiced their agreement.

"I think we should jump in while the fire is hot," Carin interjected. "Laura was a good friend and I, we, want the person who did this to be caught. If we can help do that, we should. Beth has been through some things that I wouldn't wish on my worst enemy but they've been things that have helped prepare her for this. She's smart, tough, strong, and she has all of us as a resource."

Brenda, who had left during the discussion and didn't get a chance to register her opinion at the restaurant, called Carin on her cell, was filled in, and told Carin she would go along with whatever the group decided to do.

After some discussion, the group agreed upon three hundred dollars a day plus expenses as compensation for Reddy and Associate.

Since most of the group were fairly well off financially, it wasn't difficult to get agreement to share the payment of bills among them.

A little buoyed by the confidence the group had shown in her, Beth agreed to the deal that would begin the following day. Conflicting feelings of sadness at the death of a friend, and euphoria at the prospect of beginning their best paying job yet ate at Beth as she got into her car and called Damien to deliver both bad and good news.

Having never met Laura, Damien didn't harbor the same personal connection to, or sorrow in, her death, but his heart went out to Beth when he heard the pain in her voice as she relayed the sketchy information she had learned about Laura's murder. Getting their first substantial job was not much consolation to him when he considered that the victim, the reason for the job, had been Beth's friend.

His meeting had gone well with the officials of the Kahler Hotel, resulting in another contract to teach Krav Maga classes in the basement. Luckily, the classes wouldn't start for another month so it wouldn't immediately interfere with their new job.

A tinge of anxiety struck him as he thought of taking on something as serious as a murder case, especially one that involved a friend of Beth's. What the hell did they know about investigating a murder? Nothing! But, to be honest, they needed the money; and getting their feet wet frightened, excited, and intrigued him.

While growing up in western Montana, he had never considered the possibility of becoming a PI. He had drifted after earning a college degree in business administration, never really excited about the idea of getting a job in business; he had chosen this major in college because he really couldn't think of anything else at the time, and his parents expected him to go to college. He had received his degree, along with a minor in psychology, from Missoula Western College, the latter of which he now thought could pay some dividends in his new, chosen profession.

Although now only twenty-eight years old, he had held many job titles over the past seven years: short order cook, carpenter, cowboy, and boxer, which eventually had spurred him on to studying martial arts. That was how he had become involved in Krav Maga, eventually rising to the level of instructor, which now gave him an enhanced feeling of security in his new profession as a private investigator. He was also glad that Beth was proficient in Krav Maga. If the need ever arose to use their fighting skills during the course of an investigation, he felt confident they could handle just about anything. And if that didn't work they were both licensed to carry a firearm. They had opted for nine mm Glocks; a little boom-boom was a good backup plan, he thought.

Damien pulled the Ford Focus into the attached garage. Beth, who had been waiting, hugged him as soon as he entered the house. She pulled back suddenly, "You know what, Laura Walters had been a friend of mine, but when I was pacing the floor waiting for you, I realized that I only saw her at book club meetings interacting with other book club members. Laura's husband or adult children were never there, so at least to my knowledge, no one in the book club really knew them. It just hit me as to how little I really know about her."

"Wow, right to the point. Looks like we're jumping in quickly." He shrugged and walked to the kitchen where he grabbed a beer from the refrigerator. Damien took a swig, and said, "Well, since we're going to talk about this now we might as well discuss the spouse, since they are always a suspect in any murder investigation. We probably shouldn't discount the possibility of him being the killer in this case."

"I'd agree, but, shifting gears just a little, I'm wondering about contacting the police and explaining that we've been hired by Laura's book club friends to look into this. I wonder what they'd say?" Beth looked at him, obviously requesting his opinion.

Not disappointing her, Damien said, "I'm guessing they'd tell us to stay out of it. Why would they want PI's possibly messing things up, especially as inexperienced as we are? We're probably best checking around on our own for now, and if we come up with anything of importance we could bring it to them."

Turning away slightly she considered what he had said and then replied, "It just seems like we should coordinate with them."

"I'm not saying we shouldn't, but maybe not right away, or at least until we find something useful. The police would probably be more accepting of us if we brought something important, but you're the lead person and I'll do what you think is best."

Beth chuckled to herself a little. She hadn't thought of herself as the lead PI in this business arrangement, but if that was the way Damien looked at it, she wasn't going to argue the point.

"I think you're right. They probably wouldn't accept us with open arms because we're not established and really have no credibility other than our paper licenses. Not much to go on for them to want our help. We've had two cases that were not exactly good reference points."

"We should do a Google search on her husband. What was his name again?" Damien asked.

Beth replied immediately, "Scott, Scott Walters. While we're at it, we should get the names of the adult children and do Google searches on each of them. As far as we're concerned, everyone is a suspect when you have no leads to go on."

"I'm guessing the children's names should be under Scott's information. Let's go into the office and get started on the computer."

They moved to the office, with Beth sitting in front of the computer as Damien peered over her shoulder. She began the search and soon had four Scott Walters listed. They zeroed in on the obvious one, the Scott Walters who lived in Rose Creek, Minnesota. Evidently, Scott was a real estate agent who doubled as a volunteer fireman. Laura was identified, and their three children were listed as: Robert, Alan, and Leticia. All were now adults and ranged in age from twenty-four to thirty-one.

When they did a search for each of the children, they found out that none lived in Minnesota. Robert was the closest, living in Chicago. One lived in Denver and the other lived in Los Angeles. They decided they would do some checking and find out if any of the children were back in the state visiting. They split their time and started with contacting the book club members to see if anyone knew if any of the children were back in Minnesota.

Damien got lucky on his second phone call. This one was to Kassidy Medicreek, who immediately told them she knew the family well. She related that she knew for a fact none of the children had returned to Minnesota during the last three months. She said that there was no way any of the children would do anything like this, and that Scott could never do it either.

Beth knew that although this wasn't in the slam-dunk category for eliminating them as suspects, in her mind it seemed close.

"We can't just eliminate them because someone says they would never do that," Damien said. Beth shrugged and conceded his point, but until they came across some damning evidence, she wasn't going to seriously consider the husband or children as suspects.

"Hey, you feel like taking a ride?" Beth asked Damien.

"You want to go to Rose Creek, don't you? I was thinking the same thing."

Beth spoke again, "We can talk to the neighbors and see if they know anything of interest, cruise the town, and just try to dig up some leads."

"Let's go. Might as well do our gum shoe routine and see if we can do it without ticking off the police."

"That's probably going to happen no matter what we do. So let's go," said Beth.

Chapter 3

Claude finished cleansing and drying off his body. He had taken thirty minutes to accomplish both tasks. He dreaded opening the door and still finding her in his bed, but little choice was left to him. Turning the light off first, he cracked the bathroom door slightly. His eyes slowly adjusted to the darkened room revealing an empty bed with it's coverings cast aside.

A flicker of hope that she was gone flashed through his mind and his eyes brightened as he contemplated the possibility. After opening the door fully, he ventured into the room, visually exploring it carefully in every direction as he walked toward the ruffled bed.

The bedroom door was ajar. He had closed it when he had gone to bed, but of course she had opened it when she entered later. It was obvious to him that she was nowhere in the bedroom, so she was either in the living room or gone. Moving cautiously, he passed through the partially opened doorway, entering the living room with some trepidation. A creak in the flooring greeted him as he stepped into the opening. Freezing in his tracks the instant he heard the sound, his eyes scanned the dark interior of the outer room. A sigh of relief escaped him as he realized she was no longer in his apartment.

Claude quickly moved to the entrance door to see if it was locked. It wasn't. He turned the handle and this time, hooking the safety chain to the jam, he fully secured it and breathed easier. He flipped on a lamp, pulled a notebook from the desk drawer, and scrawled himself a sloppy note: Change locks tomorrow. He would make sure that she never gained entrance to his apartment again.

Sleep appeared to be a commodity he wouldn't achieve tonight as he drifted into thoughts of how in the hell he had ever met and befriended "Kristen," though he was sure that was not her real name.

They had first met at a bar on the outskirts of Rochester. He thought the name was Whiskey Creek, but he couldn't be sure. He, along with friends, had frequented several drinking establishments that evening and he really couldn't be sure at which place he had met Kristen. Once they had hooked up his friends had left him, correctly believing that he would be involved for the evening, which he was.

Kristen was quite pretty, maybe a little older than he, and certainly as tall as he was. She laughed easily and appeared to be very interested in him. It was an easy pick up. The more he thought about it, however, the easy pickup had been him, not the other way around; it was like she had chosen him and he had gratefully acquiesced.

They had ended up at his apartment where she practically tore his clothing from his body. It was as if she had an unquenchable thirst for him. During their first weeks he had totally enjoyed being the object of her obsessive lust.

They saw each other on a weekly basis for two months. As he came to know and expect what she was going to do to him, the red flags began standing out a little more clearly. They didn't make love; it was animal sex with no kissing or foreplay. Her demeanor was always calculated and the conversation was nonexistent, far different from their first night together.

A real fear within him had begun to take hold, and he began pulling away and not answering her calls. This dominating fear that crept up his spine couldn't be explained by just one experience or comment that she had or hadn't said. It was just...a feeling, a general feeling that something was not right with her, that she was an unusually damaged human being who was fighting demons that she would never understand. He cringed when he thought of her and what she might be capable of doing. Tomorrow! Tomorrow the lock would be changed; he would make sure of that, for he wanted nothing to do with her ever again.

The previous evening had been a long one for Cadence Pieson, topped only by the disturbing book club meeting the following day at the Oak Grill. Cadence could feel the exhaustion in her body dragging her down; her eyelids felt as if they were being pulled shut by concrete blocks. She thought she shouldn't be needing these little afternoon naps to catch up on her sleep. After all, she was only forty-five years old and in good physical shape. She had been a certified physical therapist during her working days, but due to her husband's once well paying job at a brokerage house in Albert Lea, had been able to quit the profession six years ago to concentrate on her golf career.

His income could pay all the bills and still provide a membership at the local country club where she could hone her skills, give lessons, and make connections with possible sponsors across the country.

He provided her one other benefit. He traveled a lot. Sometimes she went with him so she could golf in another location at a particularly attractive golf course, but sometimes it suited her needs to stay home and do other things.

There was no doubt she was an excellent golfer, winning several amateur titles in Minnesota and across the nation. Only question lingering in her mind: Was she good enough? She hoped to gain the answer during the next two years as she practiced every spring, summer, and fall day she could in Minnesota, and winter days in Florida. She would enter a minimum of fifteen tournaments during that time with the ultimate goal of qualifying for the Ladies' Professional Golf Association Tour. She was very aware that her age limited her window of opportunity. Now was the time to concentrate on her craft and pursue her dream.

After next month's book club meeting she would be returning to her Florida home on a golf course and place a huge emphasis upon improving her short game. But first, she would have to wrap up at least one huge task in Minnesota.

Beth and Damien climbed into the Focus to begin their drive to Rose Creek, about thirty minutes away from their Stewartville home. Damien assumed the driver's seat after Beth chose to be a passenger for this trip. They had made several, previous forays to the graveyard not far from Beth's old house in Rose Creek to visit the site where her parents were buried.

Also, every year, she and her younger brother, Mark, laid a wreath at the base of their parents' graves and then went out for breakfast to Harry's Hash House in Rose Creek, their parents' favorite restaurant in town, albeit, the only one. Every time they were at the restaurant they would play a game of recognizing and naming old neighbors.

Sometimes, they thought they could hear their parents laughing at them as they stumbled in their efforts to say or remember the names of some of the locals. They had to laugh along at that point, as they always came up with some doozies in their attempts to remember names such as Feudor, an old Finnish man who was quite famous in the region for leading the St. Urho's Day celebration.

People in the restaurant usually paid no attention to them; they seemed like just a young couple having a good time, and Mark and Beth liked it that way. They really didn't want to bring up old memories or relationships. Their lives now were where they wanted them to be. Let the past be the past...to a point.

Damien entered the town from the westside, clinging to Highway 56 like they were wed to it. The municipal bar was on the left hand side of the road, just like it used to be, and still open. The Focus slowed to forty-five miles per hour, as the speed limit sign demanded, while they rounded the big curve. They slowed further and turned onto the second right, entering a small residential area. In just three blocks they came to County Road 4 passing by Laura's house which appeared to be empty.

A block after taking a left onto County Road 4 they turned on the next street, back toward Highway 56; the street where Laura had been killed. Yellow tape still identified the sidewalk area as a crime scene. After parking a third of a block away on the opposite side of the street, they got out and walked across to take a look at the murder scene.

They stayed outside the perimeter of the tape and leaned over to examine the area, more out of curiosity than actually trying to find clues to the murder. Hands stuffed inside their pockets, they stood for two or three minutes. Neither one spoke. As Beth turned and began walking toward the house directly in front of the cordoned off area, Damien followed.

They were about to leave when an older man, about 80, finally came to the door. His shoulders were stooped and he was in obvious pain.

"Sir, my name is Beth Reddy and this is my associate Damien George. We're investigating the murder of Laura Walters last night and would like to ask you a few questions. Would that be ok?"

"I don't see why not, but I've talked to the police already. Why'd they send out a couple more? Especially someone with two, first names. Damien George? What kind of name is that?"

Damien countered, "As far as my name, what can I say? It is what it is. But to clear things up, we're not the police. We're private investigators hired by friends of Ms. Walters to help the police find her killer." In the back of his mind, he thought back to all the times when he had been teased by classmates about his name.

The old man invited them in and settled them onto the sofa. Forgetting his crack about Damien's name, the old man said, "Killer or killers?"

"Why do you say that? Did you see a person or persons last night at the time of the murder?"

"Hell no! I just wondered how do they ever make any kind of statement like they did this afternoon, that a person killed Laura. A...

person! Could've been two young kids after her money. We got some dip-shit kids around here that I wouldn't trust any farther than I could see them, which isn't too far nowadays-cataracts...I'm gonna get them taken care of next Tuesday. Anyways, I gave the names of three teenagers in town that could've done this to the police last night. Are you two working with the police?"

Beth glanced sideways Damien's way and responded, "We're coordinating with the police, yes." The old man gave a skeptical tilt of his head.

"Did Police Chief Hansen talk to you personally?" Beth asked. The old man lost the skeptical look and answered.

"No, I guess this isn't a big enough case for the chief to come down and talk to a peon like me. They sent two guys in uniforms last night and then Sheriff Lewis from Spirit Grove came over this morning and asked me a few questions."

"Does he still wear that big Stetson?" Beth asked.

"Looks like he's from Texas or some place. Christ, he's a big man. Yeah. Anyways, I talked to him for a while and told him everything I knew, which wasn't much. I never saw or heard anything. To tell you the truth, I was sleeping. I'm always in bed by nine o'clock. Gotta get my beauty sleep you know."

Neither one laughed as he looked at them, expecting them to be amused by his remark. He gave a harumph, crossed his arms and sat back, waiting for another question. When it didn't come he looked at both of them.

"You two are new at this, aren't you?" Neither one quite knew how to respond until Damien mumbled something about this being their first murder case, but that they had plenty of experience in other criminal areas. The old man cracked a little smile. "Sure thing, sonny; it shows."

"Well, we should be talking to some other neighbors. Maybe one of them saw or heard something of importance," Beth said, signaling they were leaving. Before thanking the old man, they got the names of the three teenagers he had given the police and left a card for him to call if he happened to remember anything of importance.

"You won't mind if I don't see you to the door, will you? My hip arthritis complains too much."

They assured him that it was fine and they would let themselves out.

Back in front of the old man's house, Damien said, "God, I feel like a total amateur when even an old guy like that can figure out we're neophytes."

"Did you say neophytes?"

"Yeah, it's someone new at something."

"I know what it means. I'm just really surprised that you used the word. It just doesn't sound like you."

"I told you I went to college and got good grades. Why be so surprised?"

"I guess surprised was the wrong word to use. It just didn't sound like your style of speech," she said while walking toward the next house.

"My style... I don't know what you mean by that. I've got many styles that I'm going to use during our long and glorious career as P.I.s. Just wait and see." Beth tilted her head slightly as she shot him a smiling glance, but said nothing. The ice and snow crunched beneath their feet as they carefully walked the sidewalk to the next house north of the murder scene.

Beth hadn't gotten her hand out of her coat pocket to knock before the door opened and Meghan Stoutmeir greeted them. They stated who they were and what they did, and then asked if Meghan would answer questions about Laura Walter's murder last night. The 72 year old widow of Arnold Stoutmeir told them she would help out as much as she could and invited them into her living room, leading them to a beautiful leather sofa, which felt much too cool to the touch as they sat on it.

"Would you like some coffee or tea before we begin?" Meghan asked. "I don't get very many visitors so I'd love to make you some." Damien started to decline, but Beth interrupted him.

"Coffee would be great. Just black would be fine with me."

Meghan looked inquiringly at Damien who nodded his head yes and told Mrs. Stoutmeir that he'd like his coffee black with cream and sugar if she had then.

"Of course I have them; that's the way I drink it," she said pleasantly. "You're a brave girl for taking it straight, ah, I'm sorry, what was your name again?"

"Beth Reddy and this is Damien George."

"Oh yes, that's right, I have never done a good job of listening to names. I should have remembered yours though, sir. It's unusual to have two, first names like that." Damien shrugged as if to say, what can I do?

In a couple of minutes Mrs. Stoutmeir returned with three cups of coffee perched on a metal tray that looked as if it had come from a nursing home. She first served Beth and Damien, then herself, returning to a wooden rocking chair opposite the visitors. After a little chit chat regarding background information that Mrs. Stoutmeir requested from them, Beth questioned her about the previous night's murder.

"So, please tell us what you know, if anything, about what happened last night."

"I can only tell you what I first told the policemen last night, and then the sheriff who came this morning. It's not much. First of all, I have to tell you that I'm a bit of a night owl because I have trouble sleeping. I watch a lot of TV, specifically HGTV. I love that show Love It or List It. Last night they were following an older hippie couple from Greenwich Village who told the designer...I can't remember her name...Oh, Jillian. She used to be on The Bachelor show. She's from Canada, you know. She has a cute little accent, hey." She waited for a reaction that didn't come.

"Well, anyway, I digress. Last night I was watching that show and I guess it was around 10:30 when I got a little restless and started walking around the house. I do that sometimes at night. I happened to look outside, as I often do, and I saw what I thought was a person laying on the sidewalk. I thought to myself that it's awfully cold to be out there...maybe the person slipped and knocked themselves out, so I put my coat and boots on to go help.

"That's when I found out it was Laura. I saw all the blood on the snow! And her head, her head was a mess, all caved in like that. I... I didn't know what to do. She was obviously dead, so I rushed back into the house, taking care not to slip on the ice, and called the police. I did that and not long after, the police came with their lights flashing and knocked on my door.

"Oh I tell you I didn't get much sleep last night at all. Poor Laura, I didn't think she had slipped and fallen. There was too much blood and her skull wouldn't get crushed like that from just a fall. I knew she was murdered right away. I tell you I've lived here for forty-six years and there's never been a killing in this town, never." She stopped talking and just stared at the two of them.

Knowing the answer, already, Damien asked it anyway, "And you didn't see anybody around who might have done this?"

"Not a soul," she said forcefully.

"Did you notice anyone during the daylight hours who seemed to hang around the area? Anyone that looked suspicious to you?" Beth asked.

"Not a soul," Mrs. Stoutmeir repeated.

Beth asked another question, "Can you think of anyone else who might have seen anything yesterday or last night that might be able to help us?"

The old woman assumed a thoughtful posture as she took a sip of her coffee. "You might want to ask Gerald Hodges. He picks up cans and bottles in the neighborhood. He's always out and about, all times of the day and night, in town, out of town. You can see him everywhere it seems. I think that's pretty much how he makes his living. Lord, I don't really see how he makes enough money to stay alive, but I guess people throw a lot of stuff out and they don't really mind if it's on the street or sidewalk. Probably mostly kids that do it, I suppose."

Taking out a pad and pen, Damien asked, "Can you tell us where he lives?"

"I certainly can. He lives in his mother's purple house at the eastern edge of town. You can't miss it if you just turn left on County Road 4 and keep driving until you see it on the left side. His mother's long dead and don't even ask about his father. I never knew or even saw him," she added with just a tinge of disgust in her voice. She then got another thoughtful look on her face. "Say, I just made the connection. Your mother and father were Glen and Janice Reddy, weren't they?"

Beth smiled at the recognition of her parents. "Why yes, I'm thrilled that you remember them."

"It was a sad day for all of Rose Creek when they were killed in that car accident." Mrs. Stoutmeir leaned forward and patted Beth's hand. "Your dad was my dentist. He had the most gentle hands in my mouth that I ever knew," she said with a chuckle.

"He was a gentle man all around, and a great father."

"I know, dear," Mrs. Stoutmeir said as she sat back. She seemed to hesitate a bit as she considered carefully what she was going to say next. "I've read about everything that happened to you since. It seems like nothing can keep you down, Beth. When I called you a brave lady for drinking my coffee black I really wasn't thinking of just how brave you have been in your short life. All of your troubles with your uncle, his church, that horrid preacher and his girlfriend, what was her name? Cassandra, that's right. I can't believe what you went through." She set

---

33

her coffee cup back in its saucer with a clank and said, "I'll help you as much as I can. You and your friend with two first names."

Damien choked on his coffee. When the other two gave him a concerned look, he croaked, "Went down the wrong pipe."

"Sorry about that," Mrs. Stoutmeir said.

Beth reached inside of her purse, retrieved a business card and gave it to Mrs. Stoutmeir. "We're going to interview some other people on the block now, but please don't hesitate to call us if you remember anything or see anything that you think isn't just right in the neighborhood, okay?"

Taking the card, Stoutmeir said unequivocally, "I will. Good luck you two."

Over the old woman's objections, Damien gathered their saucers and cups and took them back to the kitchen. Regardless of her vocal objections, it was obvious to both that she appreciated his actions.

Outside, as they walked the sidewalk to the next house, Damien commented, "Nice old lady. She reminded me of my grandmother."

"Wish I had a grandmother," Beth said.

"How about children, grandchildren?"

"Hey! Don't get ahead of the game, here. One step at a time." Damien shrugged his shoulders.

They interviewed five more people on the block. Two others were not home. No one, it seemed, had any answers and little idea as to who might have committed the murder. Knowing they had nothing to lose, they headed to the home of Gerald Hodges. The house was difficult to miss. It stood out in its purple glory on a corner lot: two stories and in need of repair, it was, to say the least, an advertisement for demolition.

It was five o'clock in the afternoon so they were hoping that Mr. Hodges was home for supper. They were not disappointed. He came to the door dressed amazingly well for a person of little means. He wore Docker pants, Rockport shoes, and a Ralph Lauren long-sleeved dress shirt. Pleasantly surprised at his appearance, Beth and Damien accepted his invitation to enter and were guided to the meticulously restored kitchen table and chairs. Countertops were cleared and wiped. The floor was sparkling. Dishes were put away. By all their observations, Mr. Hodges was a very neat man.

A copy of Tolstoy's War and Peace lay on the table, with a bookmark sticking out near the end. After looking around the kitchen, Beth and Damien assumed a couple of chairs.

"So, you said you'd like to interrogate me in the matter of Laura Walter's death," he began a little testily.

"Not interrogate, Mr. Hodges, just ask if you happened to notice anything different the night of the murder," Beth quickly responded.

Hodges smiled. "Would you believe you are the first to visit and ask anything? The police and sheriff never bothered with me. I gather they assumed that an old vagrant such as myself would be of no use to them." He bent his head a little, pondering his own statement. "And I suppose they would be correct...in most instances." Their interest heightened when he said the last part of the statement, just as he had wanted. "Please join me in a cup of tea," he said, instantly rising to fetch the teapot. Damien protested that they had just had two cups of coffee and needed no more liquids, but was waved off by Hodges, who busied himself preparing his most precious drink.

Following a few minutes of chitchat with his back to his guests, Mr. Hodges returned to the table with his favorite tea. Sugar cubes were optional. Beth and Damien accepted the cups and thanked him.

While passionately stirring his sugar cube into his tea, Damien stopped for a moment and asked the first question. "So, Mr. Hodges, exactly what do you know about the murder? You hinted that you knew something."

"I simply said that the police would be correct in most instances that an old person like myself would have nothing useful to report to them."

It had been a long day and Beth let out a frustrated sigh before saying, "Mr. Hodges, we're not here to play games. Laura Walters was a friend of mine and if you have any information about her death, you should share it with the police and us. If you really have nothing, please don't waste our time."

Mr. Hodges beamed as he said, "My dear, I assure you that I am not playing games. I may have something for you, but then again, I may not." Damien placed his teacup on the table.

"More games. Beth, I think we should chalk this up to a guy who wants some attention, go back into town, and stop at the municipal to see if anyone knows something there."

"My boy, that won't do you any good. Interview a bunch of drunks who play pull tabs all day and all night long?" Hodges sipped his tea as he eyed them both.

"All right, Mr. Hodges, then tell us what you mean," Beth calmly responded.

"Well, the information I have may be of use to you, but that is for you to determine. I cannot do that for you, nor should I. I travel around town every day and venture out onto the county roads and ditches in my never-ending quest for treasure, uh, aluminum cans, if you prefer. I may see things most people do not. My mind is not encumbered by work, relationships, or petty jealousies of anything or anyone, so I remember things that I've seen. I am focused." He picked up his teacup and daintily enjoyed another sip of his tea.

Beth and Damien sat in silence for several seconds, eyeing Mr. Hodges.

"Well, that explains that," Beth said somewhat sarcastically as she sat back in her chair.

He continued. "On the day in question I made my rounds, as usual, outside the city."

"It's not large enough to qualify as a city," Damien interrupted.

"Town, if you will. I was making my rounds and noticed a late model automobile, though I cannot provide the name of it to you because that type of information has never been important to me so I've not studied the differences in cars."

"What color?" Beth asked.

"Red...I believe." Damien rolled his eyes.

Hodges gave Damien a cool stare. "Being male, I am rather challenged in the area of accurately identifying colors. Crimson, ruby, scarlet, I confess that I cannot tell the difference." A slight pause occurred. Damian shifted from one butt cheek to the other.

"Go on, Mr. Hodges. We're listening," Beth encouraged.

"The car I've somewhat described to you, turned around right in front of me. It was driven by a woman with blonde hair. I saw that clearly because I was at the top of the ditch on the side of Highway 56 leading towards the city-excuse me, town of Adams. The woman did a U turn in the middle of the road and headed right back to Rose Creek. She turned onto County 4 and I made note of the fact that she turned on Laura Walter's street. It was still there when I returned to town an hour and a half later." He took another sip of tea.

"And this is important because...?" Damien asked.

"Well, that's the part you have to determine, isn't it?"

"Tell us more about the woman and the car," Beth said as she leaned forward.

Hodges eagerly continued. "When I first returned to town the car was parked a few blocks away from Laura's house. I walked by it, but no one appeared to be inside. I must confess, I was on the other side of the street so the person could have been lying low in the seat. Later, approximately an hour later, the car was gone."

"So we have a late model, red car driven by a blonde woman who parked in front of Laura's house for an extended period of time, right?"

"Correct, Mr. George," Hodges responded. Again, there was silence for several moments. The room was noiseless except for the sound of teacups scraping saucers as they finished their tea.

After she had taken a sip and placed her teacup down on the saucer again, Beth asked, "Have you ever seen the red car with the blonde before yesterday?"

"Yes, several times actually. I believe it belongs to one of the members of Laura's book club."

Damien and Beth briefly looked at each other and then returned their attention to Hodges. "And the blonde, have you seen her before?" Damien asked.

"I believe I just answered that question."

Beth straightened up. "Mr. Hodges, you should tell the police this information."

"When they approach me and ask, I will," he said cheerily.

"We'll let them know that you may have some helpful information," Damien offered.

"That would be quite alright, my boy." He smiled. "I shall be more than happy to assist."

"One more question, Mr. Hodges," Beth began. "Why do you think the woman is a member of Laura's book club?"

"Well, that's simple. The car has been present whenever there has been a meeting."

"Do you keep track of everyone in town and who they associate with?"

Hodges laughed, almost spitting some of the tea from his lips. When he recovered, he said, "I know a lot about what goes on in this town. I may not know all of the comings and goings, but I know a lot," he repeated. He finished the last sip of his tea and set his cup on the saucer. He said no more.

"Well, uh, I guess we're done here," Damien said. Beth concurred and began to collect the teacups and saucers. Hodges signaled her with a wave to stop.

"I'll take care of that. May I contact you if I remember any more details of that night?"

"You certainly may." Beth reached inside of her purse and retrieved a business card. Hodges squinted as he studied the card. She and Damien rose from their chairs to leave.

"We encourage you to contact the police with the information you supplied us," Damien told him.

"I can assure you that I will." And with that, Hodges showed them to the door and let them out.

Damien and Beth waited until they were in the car before they spoke again. "What do you think?" Damien asked.

"Only one person in our book club has a red car and that's Cadence Pieson, who also happens to be blonde. She might have had a good reason to have been at Laura's house earlier in the day, and we can sure find out."

Damien shifted in his cloth seat. "Do you want to contact her now?"

Beth started the car before she answered.

"No. Not yet. I think we should do a little more checking around here today. In spite of what Mr. Hodges said about the municipal customers, we should visit there and actually see if anyone has any information that could help us."

"Sounds reasonable to me. It's at the other end of town and on our way out." He shifted his position again.

She looked at him with a little smirk on her face. "You don't have hemorrhoids or something do you? You keep changing positions."

"No," Damian said defensively. "I've...just...been a little uncomfortable with all of this sitting today. I'm not used to it."

Beth shifted the Focus into drive and began the short journey to the local city bar.

Chapter 4

Sheriff Cooper Lewis drove his squad car past Grand Meadow on his way back to Spirit Grove. He hadn't learned a great deal during his visit to Rose Creek. The murder was hard to figure out. Was it random, an accidental killing, maybe the result of a spousal argument, planned? There were no leads. The local forensic investigators would be further examining the body and scene. Lewis knew the locals would do a good job, but he preferred that the unit from Minneapolis handle this, because more resources meant better results, in his mind. Police Chief Hansen from Rose Creek, however, felt differently; the local investigators should be the only ones to handle the case.

Fifteen minutes later he was pulling up beside his office. It was two-thirty in the afternoon. Time flies when you're having fun, he told himself. As he walked in the door, Pat was busily typing a report and barely gave him a nod. Lisa was sifting through stacks of papers on a table near her desk. It appeared she had taken everything from her desk and his, and was filing those that needed to be.

Without saying a word, Lisa looked at him expectantly.

"She was murdered all right. That was pretty obvious from the scene. Poor gal. Looks like she didn't see it coming. There were no defensive wounds, nothing to indicate she expected an attack. I'd love to get my hands on the son-of-a-bitch that did this."

"Or bitch," Pat Schminski piped up.

Lisa's head twisted quickly toward Pat.

"Sorry," Pat said and returned to her refuge, typing reports.

Returning her gaze to the sheriff, Lisa asked, "So what's your first impression, Cooper?"

"We interviewed the neighbors and businessmen in town and no one can think of a person on earth who would want to hurt Laura. Right away you think it's gotta be someone she knows. The posture of her body and lack of defensive wounds back that theory up, at least for now."

"What about the spouse?" Pat piped up again. A withering look from Cooper sent her gaze and fingers back to work.

Acknowledging the question, however, Lewis said, "That's being checked out. If he's involved we'll find out. He's got a damn good alibi, though. He was in Minneapolis presenting at a convention during the estimated time of the murder. Never say never, but he doesn't look good as a suspect."

"What's he do for a living?" Pat asked.

Responding amiably but also with a little undisguised irritation, Lewis, asked, "Would you like to take over the investigation, Pat? Then you wouldn't have to go through me for the answers."

Pat scrunched her face up and then returned to typing.

Lisa Dolcheski placed a hand on Lewis's wrist and asked, "What can I do, Cooper?"

Looking at Pat, who continued typing, Lewis answered, "Well for starters, you can check out the husband's alibi and make sure he was where he said he would be, doing what he said he would be doing at the, the..." He reached inside of his pocket and pulled out his notebook. "The Radison Hotel in Bloomington," he read. Pat stifled a giggle.

"I'll get right on it. The filing can wait." Lisa took the paper from Lewis and searched for the phone number.

"I want you to go up there and interview people directly. Take a couple of days and be thorough. We want to rule him in or rule him out." He pinned a photograph of Scott Walters on the bulletin board.

"I'll pack some clothes and head up there now."

"Keep a level head, Lisa," he said quietly while gently putting a hand on her shoulder.

She looked at him, nodded, and then walked out of the office to go home and pack.

The drive to Bloomington took Lisa two hours. After parking her car, she got out and walked though the front doors of the hotel and up to the check-in desk. The clerk behind the counter greeted her enthusiastically, but assumed a serious attitude when Lisa identified herself as a deputy sheriff investigating a murder in Austin. The clerk was cooperative and referred her to the organizers of the convention, which was still in progress.

A room was available so she checked in for a day and took her duffle bag up to her room; she had packed light. After going to the bathroom and checking out her hair, she took the elevator to the second floor where the convention occupied five large meeting rooms. She spied the registration table in the center of the atrium and ambled toward it. She never noticed the short man with thinning blonde hair as he flashed in front of her, pushing a cart with a computer and other AV equipment ahead of him.

Lisa stopped abruptly as the man apologized frantically. "Sorry, I've got to get this to the Bel Air Room pronto. They had a technical breakdown and they need this yesterday. Sorry!" he said again as he rushed away. Lisa shook her head and walked a little more carefully toward the registration table, leery of any collisions that may await her.

The thirty-something woman behind the table smiled pleasantly as she noticed Lisa did not have a name tag.

"Are you here for just the second day of the convention?" she asked.

"Actually, I'm not here for the convention at all." She flashed her identification.

"Oh," the receptionist said, obviously surprised. "What may I help you with, Deputy Sheriff Dolcheski?"

"Could you direct me to the organizers of this event so that I might ask them some questions about one of your presenters?"

"Of course. They're in room 214 just behind you and down that hallway. On the right," she added, grateful that she wasn't the one to be questioned.

Lisa returned the smile, said thank you, turned and walked to the hallway. When she reached 214, the door was open and people were entering and leaving. Surveying the room, she decided to save time and ask one of the people near her about who was in charge. A portly, young man with bushy hair directed her to a gentleman sitting in a far corner of the room, intimately involved with a laptop computer.

"Sir," she began. The gentleman, who appeared to be in his late twenties, looked up, smiled, and closed his laptop.

"Hello. Are you Rita?" he asked hopefully.

45

"Uh, no, I'm Deputy Sheriff Lisa Dolcheski from Spirit Grove, Minnesota. I'd like to ask you a few questions about Scott Walters. If you're not too busy, that is."

"Oh, man, sorry. I'm expecting a lady from the hotel to help us with some technological issues we're having during the convention. It's been a bitch; breakdowns in three of the five presenting rooms. I… I… I'm having trouble keeping up with it. I'm sorry, you said Scott Walters? He had to leave early because his wife died." He shook his head. "So sad, the poor guy broke down and cried right after his presentation this morning."

"By the way, just for the record, would you please give me your name?" Lisa requested.

"Sure, sure. It's Mark Robinson. I thought you'd be in uniform, Ms. Dolacheski."

"It's Dolcheski. What time did Mr. Walters find out about his wife's death?" Lisa asked.

"I had to give him the word at nine o'clock, just after he had begun. Unbelievable! Of course he left. I personally escorted him back to his room and we even arranged a van to drive him back to Rose Creek. His car is still in the parking ramp at the hotel. You said you were from Spirit Grove? Excuse me for asking, but why is a police officer from Spirit Grove asking about Scott? The poor guy just had his wife die suddenly."

"We believe she was murdered," Lisa answered, and then added, "Not a police officer, deputy sheriff. My office has been asked to assist in the investigation."

"Uh, yeah, sorry. Murdered? Are you sure? Nobody told us that. A police chief from Rose Creek contacted us early in the morning and just said Scott's wife had died suddenly and to let Scott know as soon as possible. Actually, I guess it was a policeman in Bloomington who contacted me. Their office in Bloomington is the one that the Rose Creek police had contacted."

"We're quite sure she was murdered last night."

"Oh my God, poor Scott, I've known him for years," he exaggerated the length of time he had known Walters. "This is just unbelievable. The poor guy. He didn't know that before he left here. We all thought maybe a heart attack, aneurysm, something like that, you know? That would be tough enough, but murdered! That's wicked bad," he added. "Why did it take the police so long to contact us?"

"The police had a little difficulty tracking Mr. Walters down." Proceeding with her questioning, Lisa asked, "Do you know Mr. Walter's whereabouts last night from approximately nine p.m. to one in the morning?"

"Uh, yeah, for part of that time anyway. We had a get together with all of the presenters at 9:30, right in this room. Scott was here from the time we began to at least eleven, I think?"

"You think?"

"Well, I can't be sure, but it seems that I talked to him around that time. You're welcome to ask some of the other people who were there. Several of them are here now. Would you like me to introduce you?"

"Yes, that would be helpful."

Robinson walked her over to a couple of presenters who were relaxing between sessions and introduced her. Dolcheski went through the proper motions with them, but knew this wasn't going to result in anything anyway. She would make some routine calls to all the right people, relax, think, and then go home and report to Sheriff Lewis.

Derrick Hansen hung up the phone. He had just finished talking with Rue Shanahan, Austin Chief of Police. Technicians had been checking for any fingerprints on the body. Hansen had known it would be a long shot, but it didn't appear that prints would be recoverable, although the technicians were doing everything they could think of to make it happen.

The classes he had attended always reminded the authorities that human skin presented unique challenges. The skin may not be totally smooth, sweaty residue may be present, masking deposited prints, and they could be easily smudged or damaged during movement of the body. Time was also a significant factor, although that wasn't a problem with Laura Walter's body. She had been found within a few hours of her death. The time of year was also against recovery. Humidity helps to "activate" fingerprint residue making it more susceptible for reagent processing. Successful cases always seemed to come from humid environments in the South. The cold, less humid environment of a Minnesota winter didn't help them at all.

The investigators would attempt one long shot method of retrieving prints if their first two methods were unsuccessful. They could erect a "tent" over Walter's body and add humidity via a humidifier to attain the ideal level of 75% humidity.

Investigators were currently using magnetic fingerprint powder. This process seemed to work best if the body was only a few hours old, as Laura's body was. The powder was brushed onto suspected areas like wrists, face, ankles, necks, and any developed prints were photographed and lifted. The results wouldn't be available for several hours, but in the meantime Hansen would continue utilizing every meager resource at his disposal to find the killer.

Hansen had been informed that a couple of private investigators had been hired by the members of Laura's book club to help find the killer. He wasn't proud; he would take all the help he could get, especially when it came from Beth Reddy. He was intimately aware of her story and hoped her fledgling career would get off to a rip-roaring start in this case, although he doubted that would happen. Rue Shanahan and Sheriff Cooper Lewis had been informed of the two P.I.s' involvement and both were accepting of the situation.

Chapter 5

Beth parked the car as close as she could to the front door of the municipal liquor store. It was cold and she didn't want to experience the frigid air for any longer than she had to. They exited the car and Damien followed her through the front door of the muni. A blast of warm air greeted them as they entered the building, strolled to the bar, and deposited themselves on a couple of stools. Damien rubbed his hands together like he was trying to start a fire to keep warm.

A tall, beanpole of a man behind the bar quickly came over and asked what they needed.

They both ordered a Caffeine-Free Coke. When Damien got his wallet out to pay, Beth stopped him. "I've got this," she said. Damien smiled as he returned his wallet to his back pocket. The bartender brought the drinks and scooped up the cash. He returned about a minute later with the change.

"Say, what can you tell us about the murder last night?" Beth began.

"Are you the police?"

"Uh, no, we're private investigators hired by friends of Laura," Damien answered.

The beanpole cocked his head a little and then said, "I guess it can't hurt. I don't know much though, just what I hear in the bar."

"So tell us what you've heard," Beth said politely.

"Like I said, it's not much. People stop in, ask questions, say things. They're all searching for answers, like you two. I keep my ears open, but everything I've heard is just speculation. The people that stop in here tend to think it's the old guy that goes around collecting cans. He's out and about all hours of the day and night, always peeping in windows, doorways. He rummages in our trash and picks out all the cans. We do our own recycling here and tell him to get the hell away whenever we catch him, but sometimes he's able to sneak in, get what he wants, and sneak out. It's hard to watch for him all the time. Besides, we don't make much off the stuff anyway. At least somebody can crank out a living and clean up the environment at the same time, I guess."

"What do you think?" Damian asked.

"You mean about who did it?"

"Yeah," Damien answered.

"Well, I don't think it was the old guy. He's just a harmless old man. Anyway, I didn't even mention him to the police, but I imagine someone else has by now. I really have no idea. Probably an outsider."

"Did you know Laura?"

"She stopped in here every Tuesday night, after work I guess. She and a couple of other women would come in and always sit at that corner table right over there." He pointed to a hightop, round table big enough for five or six people to sit around comfortably. Damien gazed toward the table, observing three older men dressed in parkas and wool stocking caps, drinking Guinness Stouts. They were talking quietly and nodding toward Beth. They stopped looking and busied themselves when they noticed Damien watching them.

"Think they know anything?" Damien asked the bartender.

The bartender looked in the direction of the old men at the corner table. "You mean them?"

"Yeah."

"I doubt it, but you never know."

Beth said, "Let's find out." Damien admired this woman so much. She was smart, confident, and strong. She got up with Damien following, and walked over to the three old guys who were trying mightily not to notice the two as they approached.

Beth stood with her hands on the back of the only empty chair around the table, Damien beside her. The three old guys looked over at the same time.

"Do you mind if we join you?" Beth asked.

"Looks like you'll need another chair for Junior," said Earl, the oldest of the three. The other two chuckled. Damian grimaced a little, but swung around to the adjoining table and slid a chair next to Beth's. They both sat down.

"Could I buy you a drink, Miss?"

"You could, but I won't be needing one, sir." They introduced themselves and began asking questions. The old guys didn't appear to know anything about the murder, but came alive when the questioning turned to Gerald Hodges.

"What can you tell us about Gerald Hodges? Some people seem to think he had something to do with the murder last night."

Seth Tryton dismissed the idea right away.

"Gerry couldn't have done it. Why hell, he joins us for a drink every once in a while. Most people here may not like him much, but he's a good guy. He's a little eccentric...uh...different, but who doesn't have their little idiosyncrasies?"

Earl agreed. "I don't believe he could ever do anything like that. I'd vouch for him in a minute, if I had to."

"You may have to," Damien interjected.

"What do you mean by that?" Boston Whittley's voice rose a bit as he asked the question.

"He doesn't mean anything by that other than there are very few leads to the murder right now and, like we said earlier, lots of people in this town seem to think that he might have done it," Beth said.

"Well, people don't know what they're talking about. Gerry is just too different for people around here to appreciate," Earl said.

"And too damn smart, you could say," added Boston.

Beth and Damien were definitely getting the idea these men were friends of Hodges and would not add any incriminating information about him.

"What could you tell us about Hodges's background? Where'd he come from and how long has he been here?"

Whitley answered quickly, "He's only been around here for probably six or seven years. He took up residence in his mother's house after she died. He's told us a few stories about where he's been and what he's done. Seems like he was a Merchant Marine for several years, a Shakespearean actor in England for a while, and museum director in New York in the 90's."

Damien drew his breath in and let it out, "Impressive."

"Mrs. Stoutmeir seemed to be a little annoyed about Hodges's father. Could you tell us what you know about that?" Beth asked.

"Well, old man Hodges was a bit of a flirt and got himself into trouble with some of the ladies in and around town, if you know what I mean," Whitley winked as he took a sip from his beer. The other two chuckled.

"You think Hodges, uh, old man Hodges maybe had flirted with Mrs. Stoutmeir, and that's why she seemed annoyed?"

"Think? I know it for a fact," Earl said. Beth and Damien appeared confused. Obviously Mrs. Stoutmeir would have been quite a few years younger than old man Hodges.

"They're getting it," said Whitley to the other two.

"What you're saying is that Mr. old man Hodges had quite a thing for younger ladies at the time, right?" Damien asked as he looked at Whitley.

Whitley threw down a gulp of his drink, placed the empty bottle on the table, and said, "Yup."

"What does all of that have to do with young man Hodges, who is now old man Hodges?" Beth asked.

"Not a damn thing! You just asked about Mrs. Stoutmeir and old man Hodges," Earl said forcefully. "And another thing, Gerald Hodges isn't that old. He's only fifty something."

"But, you know what, I think that Gerald inherited his old man's fancy for younger women, especially blonds," Tryton ventured.

"Nothing wrong with that. Admiring a young, pretty woman is a decent way to pass the time, I would say," Whitley said, as he cast a lascivious eye towards Beth.

Blushing a little, Beth put her Coke down on the table. "I think we've learned enough for today, Damien. Gentlemen, you have been very helpful." She gave each of the men a card with their contact information and stood up to leave. Damien followed suit and before long they were in the parking lot.

"That was interesting," Damien deadpanned.

"Like father, like son, evidently," Beth said as she put the key in the ignition and started the car. They discussed everything they had heard this afternoon as they decided to drive into Austin and interview Cadence Pieson. Damien carefully wrote notes on his Iphone, detailing their conversations with the folks of Rose Creek.

The drive to Austin took them fifteen minutes and then another five before they pulled into the driveway leading to the home of Cadence Pieson, located on the northwest side of Austin.

"I hope she's home."

"We'll find out shortly," Beth said. The Focus rolled to a stop at the middle of the circular drive outside the entrance of the house. They exited and walked the short stretch of brushed and polished concrete pavement to the four bedroom two story home that reminded Damien of a southern mansion in Mississippi.

"Don't look so impressed, Damien. It's not that nice inside. In fact, it's pretty blah if you ask me."

"Couldn't tell it by the looks of the outside," Damien responded.

Beth rang the doorbell and fifteen seconds later Cadence Pieson opened the door, saw it was Beth, and immediately crossed the threshold to hug her. After several seconds, Beth released her hands from Pieson's shoulders to end the embrace. Pieson continued clinging to her, forcing Beth to reattach herself until Cadence was ready to relent.

"I'm so glad you stopped by. Come in and we can talk," Cadence said. Beth and Damien followed her into the atrium which was filled with natural light from the enormous skylight overhead. They crossed the room, then through a short hallway that led to a spacious sitting room. When they had settled in straight-backed chairs, Beth spoke.

She got right to the purpose of their visit. "Cadence, I have to be blunt. We have a report that identifies you as being parked across from Laura's house earlier in the day of the book club meeting. What were you doing there?" Pieson looked stunned.

"What are you talking about?"

"You were seen by a neighbor of Laura's on the day of her murder in Rose Creek, parked across the street from her house," Damien stated softly. "We need to know what you were doing there. We can't help you if you don't let us know."

Pieson didn't respond right away. "When the police interviewed me I was afraid to say anything because I thought they might have thought I had something to do with her murder."

"Go on," Beth encouraged.

"I went to see her before the meeting because I wanted her help in getting sponsors for golf this year. One of her uncles, Robby Paulsen: he owns Paulsen's Furniture in LeRoy, would back me with a ton of money if Laura would only ask him. When I asked her to just talk to him, she said no. She said she couldn't trade on family name, whatever that means."

"Your husband makes a lot on commissions, Cadence. You guys have plenty of money to go off and do whatever you want to do. Why ask for more?" Beth said.

Cadence shook her head, looking as if her life was crashing and burning. A few moments later she started crying.

"We're not making a lot of money. We're just staying afloat. Ricky has been going all over the country lately, trying to drum up investors, but people are turning away from him. I don't understand it, he doesn't understand it, but the point is we're just about broke. We can keep up appearances for a while, but we need the money! I know it's going to look bad if I say anything to the police. I can't have that happen."

"You've got to tell the police. If you are innocent there won't be any problems."

"No, I can't. It'll ruin any chance that Ricky has to recover our losses." She sniffled and took a deep breath. "If this gets out, it won't matter whether I'm innocent or not. Investors will stay away just because of the publicity and we'll never recover and I'll lose my last chance to get on the pro tour. I can't say anything, and neither can you," Cadence said forcefully.

"We can't hide this, Cadence. The police are going to find out as soon as they talk to the guy in Rose Creek who described you. They'll figure it out and you'll have to answer their questions. You can do it quietly so the press doesn't get onto it." Cadence seemed to soften and give in a little, but she cried again.

"I trust you, Beth, but if I could just wait a few hours until I can talk to Ricky about it. Can you give me that?" Damien began to shake his head no, but before he could say anything, Beth beat him to it.

"We'll give you until ten tonight, but then you have to promise to call the police, okay?" Damien turned away so neither would see his frown. Cadence initially acted like she was going to argue against the time line, but finally accepted the terms.

"Okay... I promise I'll do that. Beth, thank you so much." She began crying again.

Damien spoke, "There's one more thing. Did you ask anyone else for money, or ask someone to talk to someone about money for you?"

More tears appeared. "God, this is embarrassing," she said between sobs. "I talked to Galena Mendez. She and Chuck are rich, so I figured my good friend Galena..." she said the words 'good friend' sarcastically," would back me. "Boy, was I wrong."

"Looks like we're going to have to talk to Galena as well," Beth said to Damien, who simply nodded his head.

It was 7:15 p.m. and Damien was getting hungry, so they left Pieson's house and decided to stop at Watt's Cooking to get something to eat. Watt's Cooking was a truck stop located just off I-90 on the eastern side of Austin. Normally you could see the only large body of water located in Austin opposite the restaurant on the southern side of the Interstate, but darkness masked the view of the lake now. Austin, situated centrally in Mower County, was known as the only county in Minnesota without a natural lake. East Side Lake, and the Mill Pond in the center of town were man-made at least forty years ago.

"Do you believe her?" Damien asked as they sat down at a table for two.

"I want to believe her. She seemed desperate and scared. Enough so to maybe kill Laura? I can't wrap my brain around believing that. Obviously, we're missing a whole lot of information. I'm beginning to appreciate the job that really good detectives do."

"I agree. And after I wrap my mouth around a Super Cheeseburger we can go out and visit Galena in Seven Springs to add to our bank of knowledge," Damien said.

Chapter 6

Derrick Hansen got the word about possible fingerprints found on Laura Walter's body late in the afternoon. No identifiable prints could be lifted. The cold air and lack of humidity had guaranteed failure. It was what he thought would happen anyway, he told himself.

He grabbed his phone and got ahold of Sheriff Lewis of Spirit Grove and Chief Rue Shanahan in Austin to tell them the news. In spite of the late hour, both were still in their offices.

A brief three-way conference was held over the phone, where they discussed how they would coordinate from here on out. Near the end of the conversation, Sheriff Lewis asked if they had heard anything from Beth Reddy and Damien George. The other two answered they had not. It was decided that Lewis would contact them to gather any information they might have.

Cadence Pieson watched through a slit in the shades as Beth and Damien left her house and drove away. She rushed to her cell phone and called her husband, Ricky. When he didn't answer, Cadence left a message to call her back as soon as possible. Oh Christ, he was in Ohio, the eastern time zone. Checking her watch, she noted the time would be about 8:17 there, not too late for him. Even so, she hung up the phone and decided to leave him another message detailing the importance of calling her back before ten, Minnesota time. Sitting down on the edge of a dining room chair, her whole body shook in dread of what might happen to her if this situation sprang out of control.

She had not counted on being noticed when she had gone to Laura's house much earlier than the others. This damn red car stuck out everywhere she went. Their argument had been severe and Cadence's anger had spilled over into personal attacks against Laura. If anyone had overheard them, she would become an instant suspect. Telling the police was looking more and more like an option she couldn't afford. Beth had given her until ten o'clock before she had to contact the police. She sat, hands clasped close to her face, and fretted about what to do.

The sudden beating of bongo drums, Ricky's ring tone, caused her to nearly fall off the chair.

Lisa Dolcheski had stuck to her earlier plan and asked all the routine questions about Scott Walters. She established that several people had seen him at the party during the time period Laura had been killed. There was no way he would ever be considered a suspect in his wife's murder. He was off the hook and she would let Cooper know in the morning.

Tonight, however, she had decided she would have a little R & R, so she was now sitting in a bar near the eastern end of Highway 494 having a scotch and water. She wasn't wearing anything special, but the tight fitting stretch jeans fit her tall, lithe and shapely figure quite well. Her blond hair was now cut in a brief shag, which accentuated the pretty features of her face.

Here, she was unknown, so she could be free to do whatever she wanted. Lisa scanned the bar for any likely candidates to pick-up. Not good so far. Then, just before nine p.m., her patience was rewarded. Two handsome men, tall enough to interest her, entered the lounge and strode to a nearby spot at the bar. After observing them closely, she decided to make the first move.

Sliding seductively closer to the sandy-haired guy nearest her, she sat elegantly next to him and offered to buy him a drink. He looked her up and down and sincerely said, "You are an extremely attractive woman, but I'm not in the market for a hooker tonight." Lisa nearly choked on her drink. She couldn't contain it though and sprayed a mouthful onto the bar.

"I'm sorry, but did you say hooker? Do hookers always offer to buy you a drink?"

"Uh, no, uh, I'm sorry." He understood the rotten mistake he'd made. "It, uh, just hit me as suspicious when you sauntered over here the way you did and, uh, asked to buy me a drink. I'm so sorry...You don't look at all like a hooker. Could we start again?"

"You know what? No, we can't start again. You missed your chance, mister, and believe me, it was a chance of a lifetime for someone like you." Lisa swung her purse over her shoulder and proudly strode out of the bar muttering to herself. "Hooker? The nerve of that guy!"

Still fuming from the hooker remark, she stomped into the parking lot, determined to hit another bar and pick up someone who would appreciate the attention she showered upon them. Lisa was still seeing red and didn't notice the two punks come up behind her. She was completely taken off guard when one grabbed her wrist and upper arm and twisted brutally while the other slammed her with a forearm to the back of her head, knocking to her knees.

"Quick, drag her behind those trucks." Lisa was seeing blurred movements as they dragged, shoved, and kicked her into an area nobody could easily see. They worked quickly, trying to disentangle her purse from her arm and neck. Her mind and her strength were recovering as they continued to struggle with the straps of her purse. She began effectively resisting, which caught the punks by surprise.

"Come on, Artie, just yank it!" Lisa felt a huge pain in her shoulder as the bigger one yanked mightily and separated the bag from her body. She wasn't sure what happened next, but as she was helped to her feet, she heard soothing words and her purse was being held out to her. Lisa realized the person helping her was the guy she had attempted to pick up earlier.

"Are you okay?" Clarity returned like a fog lifting from the valley she lived in.

"Yeah, they caught me by surprise. The little bastards hit me in the back of the head when I walked out."

"We would have been here sooner, but we took too long deciding if we should follow you out to apologize once again."

"Uh, you mean so you could apologize, again," said his friend.

Lisa looked at both of them sincerely, "Well, whatever. I'm glad you did."

"I don't think they got anything out of your purse. We ran back here as soon as we saw them drag you behind the trucks. Chuck here smashed the bigger one in the mouth, making him drop the purse and they both ran off." She did a quick check of her brown, leather bag and seemed satisfied the two assholes hadn't taken anything.

"I'll call the police and get them here right away," Chuck said as he started to punch in 911.

"No need. Here comes a cruiser now." A black and white pulled into the parking lot on a routine sweep of the area. The two guys waved the officer over and began to explain what had happened. Lisa leaned up against a nearby truck and waited for the officer to come over. He offered medical assistance, which she declined, and then she showed her ID. By the time she had finished with everything, an hour had passed and she was ready to just go back to her hotel room and crash. The back of her head ached, but she felt well enough to drive her vehicle and get to bed. So much for my rest and relaxation, she thought.

"Oh, that was sooooo good!" Damien exclaimed to Beth as he finished the last bite of his burger.

"It must have been. I watched you savor every bite like it was a fantastic steak. Looks like you may be ready to visit Galena."

"You know what? It's a quarter to nine and I think we should just go home, rest, and think about this whole thing for a while. We can call Galena tonight and set up a time to talk to her tomorrow."

"Maybe you're right, Damien. We've had a long day and it would be nice to sit back in my favorite chair and digest everything we've learned." They paid the bill, left a decent tip, and hopped back in the car where Damien called Galena. They agreed upon a ten a.m. meeting at her house and she promised the coffee would be hot.

Chapter 7

Gerald Hodges left his house at precisely 7:17 p.m. He carried his giant, black, heavy-duty plastic bags for the treasure he intended to acquire tonight. He would scope out the sidewalks and streets on his way to the first stop on his list, the municipal, for any cans he would come across. This was not making him rich, but it kept him in spending money. Actually, he didn't need any more money. He just liked getting out and performing a service, as he liked to call it. He was recycling something that needed it, and he was performing a community beautification service, for which some people in town were grateful.

He knew a lot of residents in this small town viewed him with either suspicion or contempt, or they just tolerated him, but he didn't care. He had his little group of old men, where he was the youngest by probably a decade, to provide him with the conversation and intellectual stimulation that he had craved ever since his work in the museum.

Boston Whitley was one he particularly enjoyed. Seth Tryton and Earl Mancoat were window dressing for the intellectual discussions that he and Boston regularly maintained when they gathered at the municipal.

All three gentlemen had been curious about his background before he had returned to Rose Creek, and he had provided them with most of the details of his varied activities...most, anyway. They had no idea how he had really made his money or sustained his interest in life.

Indeed, they had no idea that he really didn't need any money at all. He was, as he liked to comment to his imaginary friend, set for life.

Marriage had been part of his life three times. He had charmed his way into the lives of two semi-wealthy women, who left him with tidy sums before they met their ends, for which he was almost totally exonerated, and one extremely wealthy woman whom he married for love. That didn't work out either, not in anyone's death, but in just a normal divorce. He would always yearn for Lucille, but, as he found out, life goes on and we become enamored of others through the years. No one woman could ever hope to match what he had found in Lucille, but he had come to know of one whom he hoped to persuade to fall in love with him. As far as he currently knew, she didn't even know he existed, but he knew her. He knew her well. Gerald had watched her, followed her, admired her, listened to her speak on at least a monthly basis, sometimes even more often, such as the day she argued with Laura Walters. Someday he would walk up to her, introduce himself, and let her know the depth of his feelings for her.

Highway 56 completed nearly a half circle around the northern outskirts of Rose Creek as it wended its way on through Adams, LeRoy, and then ended at Highway 63. Mr. Hodges had to wait for several cars to pass before he could cross to the other side and sneak up on the dumpsters behind the municipal to collect a multitude of aluminum cans and whatever else he could find that he could recycle and sell. Along the highway, particularly on the northern side, he retrieved half a dozen cans strewn at regular intervals it seemed. He wondered if someone was playing games, trying to set them apart at precisely the same distance.

Oftentimes he would entertain himself with such silly notions to keep his mind occupied, for he didn't want to let his brain become a wasteland of zero thoughts and ideas. Sometimes he would try to work out mathematical equations in his head as he stalked the ditches and roadways, ever mindful not to let any thought or idea go unchallenged. He needed to be active. He needed to be challenged.

Because he had been yelled at before by the beanpole, who always seemed to be working and keeping an eye out for him, Hodges approached the dumpster warily. Unlike me, he probably needs the money, he told himself, feeling generous in his assessment of the young man.

Tonight, no one bothered him as he rummaged through the trash, including left over pizza, french fries, wrapping papers, and other assorted paraphernalia. Finding what he wanted wasn't always easy when he would end up lowering his body halfway into the dumpster to retrieve what he wanted, scraping leftover food and sometimes a little beer splash onto his jacket. Not a glamorous job, but it made him feel useful and happy to be doing something beyond the usual lateral thinking exercises he had gotten out of some book he'd found at a garage sale.

Hodges was fifty-five years old, although to most, he seemed older. His brown/gray hair was shorn down to the skin on the sides with longer strands left on top; there was plenty of it left to comb over a small, balding spot on the back of his head. A little wheat belly led him around to wherever he roamed on his medium, six foot frame. Slightly hunched as he walked, he looked unremarkable, but felt special, unique, although he had no need for people to think of him that way. Secure in his own self-image, as he had stated to Beth and Damien, he did have no petty jealousies, work, or relationships to fret about, although he was working on that last one.

Hodges smashed each can with his left foot-always his left, because he could be a man of obsession. At one time, many years ago, a silly doctor had diagnosed him with Obsessive Compulsive Disorder. Now, he just thought of himself as knowing how things should be done. There was always a right way to do things, and he always did everything the right way.

The cans were thrown into his bags and twist tied exactly six inches from the top. He slung a bag over each shoulder and began the cold walk back to his place. He made it easily across the highway, between passing automobiles, and trudged slowly through the little town until finally slipping into the garage and depositing the bags with several others lined up perfectly against the north side of the wall. Taking off his dirty coat, he hung it on a hooked nail next to the door entering the house. His boots came off next and were placed below his coat, lined up so that the toes faced the wall and the laces were tucked inside the boots so they didn't get wet when clinging snow melted.

He cast an admiring look at his treasure bags lined up against the wall. Hodges took pride in the extra money he took in from the aluminum cans, even though he had no need of such money.

Tomorrow he would load them into the bed of his truck and take them to Dubinskie's, a recycling center in Austin, which always paid him top dollar for his haul. A self-satisfied sigh flowed from his lips and then he turned and softly walked into his home.

Everything was as he had left it, in its proper place, neat. Life was so grand. Tea and a bowl of soup were on his agenda, so he began to prepare both: chamomile tea tonight, along with vegetable soup made with carrots, corn, and green beans from his own garden. For added bulk, he dropped a handful of chicken he had diced up earlier in the morning.

He worked steadily preparing the evening meal, content in every way but one. The woman he secretly admired knew nothing of his feelings and that nagging thought bothered him. But that would change when the time was right. He would just have to bide his time and be patient. Hodges smiled, because he was good at that.

In a few minutes the soup and tea were both hot. Hodges dug in with relish, one hand resting on his knee below the table and the other holding the spoon with which he fed himself. His parents had taught him how to eat properly. Never put an elbow on the table and always say please and thank you.

When he finished eating, he immediately washed the dishes by hand, dried, and put them away in the cupboard where they belonged. The dish towel was folded neatly and hung in its proper place on the handle of the stove. The countertop was wiped clean and he inspected the floor for any errant drips or particles of dust that the forced air furnace may have deposited. Grabbing the mop, he swabbed the floor like the Merchant Marine he used to be.

He made a note to himself to have the furnace men visit next week and clean all the ductwork. They had last visited two months ago and his sensitive nose was beginning to be bothered by dust mites again. Infernal creatures!

Hodges had looked them up in his ancient encyclopedia and recoiled at the thought of those nasty looking little creatures attaching themselves to dust and then entering his nasal passages. Crossing to the other side of the kitchen, he retrieved his filtered mask and put it on. He could breathe easier now.

Cadence Pieson fumbled and then answered her cell phone.

"What the hell is so important that I'm supposed to call you before ten? I've got clients lined up 'til midnight and only have a few minutes. What's going on?"

"Ricky, you won't believe what's going on," she said, nearly running out of breath. She went on to explain the entire situation, including her visit and subsequent argument with Laura about the sponsorship the day of the murder.

"I don't know what to do. Beth Reddy and her friend, Damien George, were here an hour and a half ago and she said I should go to the police by ten o'clock tonight. I finally agreed to do it, but, but I don't want to." Ricky was silent on the other end of the line.

"Ricky, Ricky, are you still there?" She was getting frantic.

"I'm here," he said loudly. "I just have to think about this. We've still got a little over an hour before you said you'd contact the police. One thing, Cadence, you've got to tell me: Did you kill Laura?" She almost dropped the phone.

"I can't believe you just asked me that. Of course I didn't," she said vehemently.

"I'm sorry. I'm sorry. I can't believe I asked it either. I'm sorry! You could never do something like that." More apologies followed.

"Did Beth say she would go to the police if you didn't?"

"No. Not really. She just made me promise that I would talk to them by ten tonight."

"Give me her number. I'll call her right now."

"But what about your clients? You've got to get them to invest or we're, we're going to lose everything."

"We don't have a choice. I've got to talk to her now and convince her that we need more time. Maybe she'll agree to give us a couple of days."

"She said the police are going to find out anyway, that the person who told them about me will talk to them and I'll look even guiltier." There was a long tortured silence on the other end. Ricky finally exploded in anger.

"God damn it, Cadence! How do you manage to do this? First you quit your job to try and be a pro golfer and force me to work eighty hours a week trying to support you. Then you get involved in some murder investigation that jeopardizes my work and our entire lives. When will it ever end with you? You've become the anchor around my neck that's continually dragging me down farther and farther. Jesus! We might as well hang everything up. You're trapped. We're trapped." He finally quit ranting. The only sounds on the phone were his panting and her desperate crying.

Several moments later, Cadence spoke quickly but hopefully. "Beth said if I talked to the police, they might try to keep it quiet for a while so the press can't get a hold of it, and…and… maybe that could give you time to line up the investors." She listened optimistically for an agreeable word from Ricky.

"And what happens when word does get out a few days later that somehow you were involved in this whole thing? Do my investors run like they would catch the plague from me if they stayed in?" These were not the calm, agreeable words she wanted to hear from him. Somehow, she had thought it might work out. What choice did she... they, really have?

And then, after several tense moments, Ricky seemed to grab hold of himself and recover. "Look, I'm sorry. You're right. It's the best we can hope for. We've got to do it Beth's way."

A huge feeling of relief flushed over her. "Yes, yes, I knew we could figure this out, and it'll be all right. You'll see, Ricky."

"I hope so," he said, defeat in his voice. "I've gotta go now. I'm in no mood to talk to these guys right now, but I'm going to have to anyway. Go ahead and do what you've gotta do and I'll do the best I can from this end." Before he closed, he added, "Let the chips fall where they may. I'll be back in two days." They said uneasy goodnights to each other and hung up.

Ricky stared at his phone for several seconds. He regretted being cruel to her and it made no difference that he really meant what he had said. It had still been a cruel thing to say, but what was said, was said.

All he could do for now was to make his presentations to the group he was meeting tonight and hope it was good enough to make them invest, because he needed this… badly. And he hoped to hell that whatever Cadence had gotten herself into, didn't screw things up.

Police Chief Rue Shanahan received a call at home, a rare occurrence. Usually phone calls made to their home were for his wife. Checking the caller ID, he saw the name Cadence Pieson. He assumed she was contacting him about Laura Walter's murder.

"Chief Shanahan," he professionally answered.

"Hello Chief Shanahan," Cadence nervously began. "This is Cadence Pieson and I'd like to meet personally with you to, uh, tell you some things that I should have told you right away about Laura Walters." Shanahan perked up. He hoped this was an early break in the case.

"Yes, Mrs. Pieson, I can meet you at the station in about fifteen minutes, I-"

"No, no, please, no police station. I'd like to come to your home and speak with you there. Could we meet tonight?"

Shanahan hesitated and then said, "All right. Come over and we'll talk."

"Thank you, Chief. I appreciate it."

Cadence arrived twenty minutes later and was welcomed into the Shanahan household by Rue's wife, who didn't appear surprised by such a late visit. Chief Shanahan stepped from the living room to greet Cadence.

Mrs. Shanahan knew this would be a confidential meeting and exited upstairs to the bedroom.

"Mrs. Pieson, I'm very curious about what you think you should have told me about Laura Walter's death. Please sit down." Pieson took a seat on the couch, but looked uneasy as she did so.

"Can I be absolutely sure that what I tell you won't be repeated to your wife?"

Shanahan answered immediately. "You don't need to worry about that. This conversation is professional, meaning I will have to share it with other law enforcement personnel involved in this case, but no one else...including my wife."

"I can't have the media aware of this either. It affects the professional and financial well-being of my husband's business and I need your assurances that this won't be spread all over town." Shanahan's posture changed as he considered her request or demand, whichever it was.

"Mrs. Pieson, I'm not going to go running to the media with the information you give to me. That being said, I can't promise you this won't eventually become public knowledge, especially if it affects the outcome of this case. And especially if you are involved in a crime."

"I am not involved in any crime," she added quickly. "But I, we-my husband and I can't have any of this in the paper or television news because it will ruin us. We're already in bad financial shape and if we, I, look like I'm involved in Laura's murder, we'll be financially and professionally crushed." She looked at him pleadingly.

He was silent for several moments and then repeated what he had said before. He added, "You've already indicated you know something that might help us in this investigation." He leaned towards her. "I will put and hold you in jail until you tell me everything you know. Now, I meant what I said when I told you I'm not going to broadcast this to the media unless you're a suspect in this crime, so, as my uncle always used to say, either shit or get off the pot." Shanahan gave her an "I mean business" stare.

Pieson blurted everything she knew in a torrent of words. He sometimes had to stop and have her repeat the garbled message, which came out haphazardly. He questioned and requestioned her, trying to piece her story together so that he was sure of her details and timeline.

An hour later, Shanahan was reasonably sure of her story and also of her truthfulness. Cadence was exhausted but relieved to have told the police chief everything and was hopeful of just going home and collapsing into bed.

"I'll share what you told me tonight with Derrick Hansen, the police chief of Rose Creek and Sheriff Lewis of Spirit Grove, and that's it for now. I'll also be speaking to Galena Mendez."

"No, no, I don't want her involved," Pieson protested.

"I'm sorry, but I need her to confirm parts of your story. We will be discreet and ask the same of Mrs. Mendez. I can't promise this will never come out to the public, but I'll do my best to keep it under wraps unless I find out that you've failed to tell me everything."

Pieson was too tired to argue anymore. She only nodded feebly and then her head drooped onto her chest.

Shanahan walked Cadence to the door and then out to her car. She drove home with a curious mixture of relief and dread in her mind, although it was more of the former than the latter. Driving home was more of a chore than she thought possible. It was if the weight of the world had been lifted from her shoulders and exhaustion was now free to overcome her. She made it to the garage and then into her house where she collapsed into bed and fell asleep almost immediately.

At 10 a.m., Beth and Damien arrived at Galena Mendez's house, a beautiful rambler with a walkout basement situated in the Seven Springs area of Austin. The countryside was different here than anywhere else in Mower County: Rolling hills, creeks, and oak trees sprinkled the land. Wild turkeys and deer roamed the three square miles that were becoming home to an increasingly large number of well-to-do families that relocated here from other upscale locations in Austin. You could still be country, although, upscale country, here.

Mrs. Mendez answered the door with a smile as Beth and Damien said hello and stepped into the grand entrance of the home. She offered them something to drink and then ushered them into a sitting area.

Galena, thrilled they had chosen to visit with her, and hungry for knowledge, asked, "How's the investigation going, have you found anything out?" Damien drew his breath in to speak, but it was Beth who spoke ahead of him.

"Well, that's why we're here, Galena." Galena looked ecstatic. "We spoke with Cadence Pieson last night." Beth quickly ran through the story Cadence had told them and waited for Galena's reaction. Bobbing her head up and down, Galena confirmed the gist of Cadence's story and told them she had refused to provide her with any promise of money. She explained that she and her husband didn't think it would have been a good thing for Cadence or her husband.

"Why not?" Damien asked.

"This is awkward, but, everyone in the book club knew Cadence had been involved with some other men and, to be frank, I wasn't going to shell out any cash for her to have a good time with someone other than her husband."

Quite shocked, Beth said, "I didn't know that!"

"Sorry, Carin was supposed to let you know, but she must have thought you couldn't handle it." Galena shrugged her shoulders and sounded apologetic.

Shaking her head and still not comfortable with the idea, Beth asked, "So was that the reason you told her that you wouldn't give her the money?"

"Oh God no! I told her that I just didn't think it would be a good idea to go off and leave her husband for long periods of time and that I couldn't play a part in separating the two of them."

"How did she react?"

"She was angry. In fact, she blew up and said it wasn't any of my business what she did or how long she might be away from her husband. I just said that I was sorry, but that was the way I felt. She stomped out of the house and hasn't spoken to me since, even at book club."

"Galena, I know that you and Cadence haven't been best of friends for a very long time. Why do you suppose she came to you for money?"

"Desperation, I suppose. Their financial troubles are not well known around town, but Nathan and I know that the Piesons are in a tremendous amount of debt. Business has gone south for Ricky and we think they're on the verge of bankruptcy."

"We found that out last night when we interviewed Cadence," Damien volunteered. Beth raised an eyebrow at Damien.

"She told you? I'm surprised. They've been hiding it very well with everyone in town, including members of the book club. Nathan and I are about the only ones that know how bad off they really are."

"Do you know if she asked anyone else for money?" Beth asked.

Galena hesitated. "I know she was going to ask Laura, but I don't know if she ever really got the chance."

"Evidently she did. They had an argument about it the day of the murder."

"Sounds like Nathan and I weren't the only ones to turn her down for money. Hey wait, you don't think Cadence killed Laura, do you?"

"No, I can't imagine it."

It was eleven a.m. when Beth thanked Galena for all she had told them, and Damien and she left to check in with Rue Shanahan at the Austin Law Enforcement Center. During the ten minute drive, Damien asked Beth if she was sure that Cadence couldn't have killed Laura.

"Never say never, I guess, but she just doesn't seem like she would be capable of such a thing."

Damien pressed his point further, "They were in debt up to their eyeballs and she was probably really angry with Laura when she was turned down again. Any person can do something crazy if pushed to the breaking point. I'm not saying she was that far gone, but it is at least possible she killed Laura."

Beth was at a loss for words. Pulling into the parking lot of the law enforcement center a little too fast, the car slid sideways and almost slammed into an old Chevrolet parked near the entrance.

"Whoa, that was a close one!" Beth said excitedly. Damien opened his eyes and unclenched his teeth.

"Yeah, we'd better get in there. Shanahan's probably chomping at the bit to find out what we know. I hope Cadence followed through and let him know the details of the other day."

They said nothing as they walked briskly through the parking lot to the front entrance of the building and then down a hallway to Shanahan's office. Along the way a couple of policemen who recognized Beth nodded and said hello.

Shanahan's door was wide open so they walked in to find him on the telephone. He signaled them to sit down in a couple of chairs across from his desk as he continued talking.

"Yeah, sure, Derrick. Now you know as much as I do about Cadence Pieson. She willingly told me what happened. In fact, she contacted me. Whether it has anything to do with the murder is another story. Hey, look, Beth Reddy and Damien George just popped in with a report, I assume." He gave each of them an expectant look. "Okay, talk to you later when I have more information. Yeah, you too." He hung up, exhaled for what seemed forever, sat back and folded his hands on his lap.

"What do you two have for me?"

They both began to speak at the same time. They stopped and both started again. Damien looked at Beth. "Okay, you talk."

Beth recounted their interviews yesterday with the residents of Rose Creek, Cadence Pieson last night, and this morning with Galena Mendez. Shanahan appeared to be preoccupied as he listened, but it was clear he had heard every word by the time Beth had finished.

"I'm glad you advised Cadence like you did. She came over to my house last night and told me everything exactly like you said. I've given all the details to Derrick Hansen and Cooper Lewis in Spirit Grove to keep everyone up to date." He leaned forward and looked at Beth. "I guess it helps to know some of the people who were close to Laura, like you do. It doesn't make it easier on you, but gathering information and putting it together like you have shows me and the others that you two know what you're doing, and we appreciate your help."

By the time Beth and Damien left Shanahan's office they felt as if they were valued members of the team, loose and unofficial members, but nonetheless, part of the team.

Chapter 8

The next morning, Lisa Dolcheski called Cooper Lewis, lied about needing another day to continue to check out Scott Walter's story and then hung up. She needed another day, all right, but not for anything involving Scott Walters. Tonight she was going back to the bar where she had been mugged and see if the two bastards showed up again. When they did, there'd be some payback.

Meanwhile, to kill some time, she visited every nook and cranny of the Radisson Hotel she occupied, including the Caribou Coffee shop, which was tucked into a corner spot on the first floor. Then she actually bought a swimming suit and did twenty laps in the hotel pool. After her swim, she enjoyed a great, blackened chicken sandwich on ciabatta bread at the nearby TGI Fridays.

The evening finally came and she couldn't wait. She made sure she had what she needed in the trunk of her car and drove to the bar.

The parking lot was fairly well lit, so she parked in a far corner that was a little darker than the rest of the lot and waited, periodically running the engine to keep herself warm. A couple of hours went by without any action, then another two hours. Nothing happened, except the movement of customers in and out of the bar. She knew it would be a long shot that the creeps would actually return after their last experience here, but she was counting on their stupidity to bring them back, so she waited, and waited some more.

Her patience was rewarded around 12:20 a.m. when she noticed an older Ford F-250 drive slowly through the lot and park on the side farthest from where she waited. Two individuals occupied the truck for another minute. Both exited the vehicle and hung out in the shadows not far from the entrance to the bar. A smile spread across her face as she retrieved her tool, being careful to keep it close to her side as she walked across the parking lot toward the assholes.

She whistled a slow tune her father used to play on his records when she was growing up. As she came closer to her targets they withdrew deeper into the shadows of two nearby SUV's. Got a little surprise for you boys. She continued walking their way as she smugly enjoyed thinking of what she was going to do to them.

She passed them by. Lisa knew exactly where they were and could hear their footsteps as they hastened towards her. When they were just feet away, she whirled around and caught the bigger one on the side of his head with the nightstick, dropping him instantly in a heap. The other shocked punk attacked her in anger, making himself an easy target for her next swing. The backhanded blow caught him in the neck, throwing him to the ground in painful agony, pitiful whimpers escaping from his lips.

The two lay moaning, stupidly talking trash, calling her an Amazon bitch. Big mistake boys. She swung the stick, giving the big one a shot in the ribs.

"God damn it, you fucking whore!" he said as he curled into a fetal position. She swung again into his ribs. This time nothing came out of him except moans. The smaller one kept quiet, but she gave him a crack on his left knee. She thought a moment, and then gave him a crack on the other knee. She didn't think she broke anything, but she was sure he would be sore for a few days. Both whimpered and cried like babies.

She was lucky, she observed; no one else was in the parking lot. As far as she knew, no one had seen this little episode. Feeling good about her evening and relishing the payback she had delivered, she held the nightstick close to her side and began walking to her vehicle. The little one moaned something. She thought it had something to do with her sexual orientation. Moving back quickly, she stood over him threateningly.

"I'm sorry, I didn't get that last part. What did you say?" He spat at her and repeated the slur.

She shook her head. "My God you two are stupid." She delivered another blow to one of his knees. This time she heard a sickening, crunching noise upon contact. Hmm, I think I broke his patella. Too bad. More moaning ensued. She made it all the way back to her car this time. Time to go home. She hummed upbeat tunes while driving slowly back across town to the Radisson. This was a good night, she said to herself.

Early the following morning she drove back to Spirit Grove to apprise Sheriff Cooper Lewis of everything she had found out about Scott Walters. Of course, everything she found out affirmed his story, which she expected, but it had been a good two days that had ended in the culminating event of last evening. She relived the moments. It wasn't often that an officer of the law got to pummel some scumbags like that. God, it felt good.

Pulling into her parking area near the office, she calmed herself. She couldn't go into the office wearing such a smug, happy look on her face. Taking a few moments to come down from her high, Lisa felt she had composed herself adequately and exited the vehicle.

Pat Schminski had just finished filing reports and turned around in time to greet Lisa as she stepped through the doorway.

"How was the trip to The Twin Cities? Find out anything incriminating on Scott Walters?" Pat's tone of voice was anxious.

Cooper Lewis jumped in before Lisa could respond. "Pat, Lisa and I are going to sit down in the conference room and discuss this. Could you please run down to the gas station and bring us some Cappuccinos?" Pat rolled her eyes as she moved to the coat tree and put on her coat.

"I keep telling you, Cooper, they're not real cappuccinos; they're fake. Real cappuccinos don't have all that sugar in them and they don't taste as good." She buttoned her winter coat, slamming the door on her way out.

The "conference room" was the back corner of the slightly over-sized office with a round, wooden table surrounded by six chairs.

"Okay, whadda ya got?" Cooper asked.

"He didn't do it. I interviewed everyone there who had contact with him the night she was murdered and there's no way he could have made it back to Rose Creek and killed her in the time frame the coroner gave us. The last anyone saw him was at an after-hours party for presenters. He was seen walking to his room just before 1a.m. The old lady, Stoutmeier, found Laura on the sidewalk around 1:30 a.m., didn't she?"

"Yeah, that's about right. Looks like we can strike him off the list."

"Well, he never was a strong suspect anyway," Lisa said.

"On the plus side, we do have another possibility," Cooper began.

Lisa, surprised, asked, "Who?"

"A member of the book club named Cadence Pieson. Rue Shanahan let me know about her last night." He explained about Pieson and the story she gave the Austin police chief.

"And you, Hansen, and Shanahan believe her story?"

"None of us are sure, of course. All three of us are paying a visit to Mr. Gerald Hodges tomorrow morning to find out if he knows any more than Ms. Pieson has divulged. We have looked into the Piesons' finances, and she has told the truth about that. By the way, you're going with us." Lisa smiled when she heard this.

"What about Spirit Grove? Do we leave it defenseless?" she said sarcastically.

"Hardly, Randall Johnson, our sometime volunteer deputy will be watching over our fair town tomorrow while we're gone."

Lisa had completely forgotten about Randall, probably because they never used him. He had gone through the training two years ago but never been called upon to do anything other than keep his training up to date, which he had. Like other small communities that could only exist because of volunteer firemen, Spirit Grove had carried the volunteer process a bit farther than most with the training and hiring of a seldom-used volunteer deputy sheriff.

Randall's regular job was as a self-employed carpenter, which gave him vast flexibility in terms of hours available for duty. He would be thrilled to finally perform the functions for which he had aspired and been trained in. It also didn't hurt his bottom line that he would be paid the going rate of $150 per full day each day that he worked for the county. Volunteer did not mean strictly "volunteer:" He would be paid for his fill-in duties as Deputy Sheriff of Spirit Grove.

Gerald Hodges's alarm blew up at 6:15 a.m.-not exactly blew up, but made the sound of a building being ignited and imploding. He loved waking up to the glorious noise of an explosion and the resulting crumbling and rumbling of a building being destroyed. There was something about the orderliness of the sequence of events that caressed and reassured his mind that all was right with the world. He thought of it as a transcendental experience, and it sent him into an ecstatic, exuberant welcoming of the day ahead.

Today he would be visited by a cadre of law enforcement personnel that would interview him, pick his considerable brain, and possibly even try to implicate him in the murder of Laura Walters. He looked forward to the encounter.

After the three s's-shit, shower, and shave-Gerald dressed himself in the clothing he had laid out the night before when first informed that he would be visited by the "dynamic" team of investigators assembled by the local powers. He had chosen a purple, long-sleeved shirt; cream colored, pleated khakis, tan dress socks; brown, suede loafers and a tan sports coat with elbow patches. God, he loved his elbow patches. He had even considered use of an accessory, the long, black pipe his father had smoked, but he didn't really care for the smell of smoke so he rejected the idea, although it was a tough decision, because of its well used elegance. It had a large bowl and a perfectly smooth airway from the draft bowl to the end of the mouthpiece. He could just see his father smoking that pipe in the evening, blowing smoke rings into the air and piercing them with the back scratcher that he carried with him every evening. Gerald could spend hours watching his father smoke that lovely pipe, enthralled with the entire process of smoking. The only bad part of the experience had been that he eventually realized he was allergic to the smoke, and try as he might, was unable to overcome his abhorrence of ingesting it into his lungs.

He considered a hat, thought that a little too pretentious, and then a tie, yes, a bow tie. He had a plethora to choose from.

Hodges rushed to the bottom drawer of his dresser where they were kept. Pulling out several at a time, he finally decided on the darker purple that he would have to tie himself. The process of assembling a knot for his bow ties fascinated him. First, he placed the bow tie around his neck, situating it so that the longer end was precisely two inches below the other then crossed the longer end over the shorter. He would then bring the longer end up and under the loop and double the shorter end over itself to form the front base loop of the bow tie. Next, he would loop the longer end over the center of the loop just formed. Holding everything in place, he would double the longer end back on itself and poke it through the loop behind the bow tie. Finally, he would adjust the bow tie by tugging at the ends of it and straightening the center knot until it was perfect; it had to be perfect.

He straightened it as he watched himself carefully in the mirror and smiled at the vision he presented. Walking gracefully to the kitchen table, he seated himself in a straight-backed chair and waited for his guests with a hot cup of tea resting between his palms.

Hodges did not have to wait long, for he had timed everything to the minute. Of course, the only event that could have spoiled his timing was an early or late arrival of his guests, but that didn't happen. He smiled and rose from his chair when he heard the doorbell ring.

Derrick Hansen was the first to be cheerily met, then Chief Rue Shanahan, and lastly Sheriff Cooper Lewis and Deputy Dolcheski. Each was given a hearty handshake by Hodges and a so glad to see you greeting. He then showed them into his abode and directed each one into a specific chair he had decided upon earlier.

"Mr. Hodges," Hansen began, "first off, we'd like to apologize for not interviewing you earlier in the process, but-,"

Interrupting, Hodges said, "No need to apologize, my boy. I'm just an old garbage collector who doesn't get noticed much around the community."

Rue Shanahan seized the opportunity to speak. "Mr. Hodges, we understand that you have some information that could help us solve this case rather quickly. We'd like you to begin with the day Laura Walters was murdered and tell us what you had told Beth Reddy and Mr. George. And if you have remembered any further details of that, or previous days, we would be very interested."

"Ah yes, the pretty, young Ms. Reddy and the gentleman with two, first names." He tugged at his bow tie a little. "I remember them well. Charming couple, wouldn't you say?" The men collectively nodded, as did Lisa Dolcheski. Gerald Hodges proceeded to relate the entire story he had told to Beth and Damien. The four law enforcement personnel hung on every word. With Hodge's consent, Shanahan was recording the story.

When he had finished, Sheriff Lewis asked, "How do you know so much about the book club and the women that meet?"

"Well, Sheriff Lewis, I am not acquainted with each woman who has attended the meetings, but they have been holding regular conferences at Ms. Walters' home for several years now. During my wanderings around town, seeking garbage for resale you understand, I have become familiar with faces and vehicles that are different from the norm in Rose Creek. Surely, you can understand that?"

Lewis graciously countered, "Of course we can, Mr. Hodges. I like to think of myself as a phenomenal observer of people, as well."

Hodges was delighted with Lewis and hurriedly said, "Yes, in your profession you must have that bent. I respect that."

Derrick Hansen asked, "Do you ever attach names to the women you have observed at the book club meetings?"

Hodges sat back and appeared to be puzzled by the question. "I just don't know how I could ever know any of their names, unless I overheard them as they entered or departed, but I have heard a few first names, and I didn't tell Ms. Reddy this, but I did recognize her as one of the book club members when she interviewed me earlier with her Mr. George. She is quite beautiful and hard to... not notice." Again, the men nodded while Dolcheski maintained a masked expression on her face.

"Earlier in the day you had noticed Ms. Pieson's car in town," Cooper Lewis stated.

"So that is her name. Bravo! You have tracked her down quickly. I am impressed with your marvelous detective abilities, gentlemen…And lady," he added.

"Had you ever noticed Ms. Pieson visit Mrs. Walters at other times during the day previous to the night of the murder?"

"Do you mean on the same day or other days?" Hodges asked.

"I'm sorry, that was a poorly worded question," Hansen apologized. "I actually meant on other days. Did you ever see Ms. Pieson or her vehicle in Rose Creek on days not involving a book club meeting?"

"I do not believe so, Chief Hansen. I don't recall ever seeing a member of the club or their vehicle at Mrs. Walters' house on a day other than the day of a book club meeting. Is Mrs. Pieson a suspect in the crime?"

Cooper Lewis answered. "She is a person of interest." And then he asked, "Where were you during the hours of 10:30 p.m. and 1:30 a.m., the evening of Mrs. Walter's murder, Mr. Hodges?" Gerald Hodges looked taken aback.

"Do you think that I may have killed Laura Walters?"

"I'm just asking your whereabouts, Mr. Hodges. We have to examine all angles."

"Of course. I'm sorry. The night of the murder I was out on my rounds until precisely nine p.m. I came back here, took a hot shower, read several chapters in a book, and actually fell asleep in bed with the book propped on my chest." He smiled widely while allowing his glance to shift back and forth amid the four individuals interrogating him. Hodges observed no telling signs of belief or non-belief on their faces.

"Mr. Hodges, could you tell us where you lived before coming to Rose Creek? My notes state that you've been around here for approximately five years." Derrick Hansen peered up from his notes.

"Actually, I returned to Rose Creek seven years ago when my mother died and left me this house. I grew up in Rose Creek, left at an early age and travelled the world, a bit of a vagabond for most of my life," Hodges revealed.

"And what did you do to support yourself for all of those 'vagabond' years, Mr. Hodges?"

"I do say, this is getting a little off course here, but in the interest of helping out the local authorities, I will tell you my life story if you desire."

"Your life story won't be necessary, but please do fill in the blanks as to what you've done and where you've been since you left Rose Creek, if you would." It sounded like a command, rather than a request from Chief Shanahan.

Some exasperation creeped into Hodges' voice tone when he answered. "All right. My father and I didn't get along well when I entered my teenage years, so when I turned eighteen I joined the Merchant Marine. That would have been about 1976. The Viet Nam War was over and I was looking for adventure, but nothing dangerous, mind you. I stayed in for twenty years and then fulfilled a lifelong dream to act, joining a Shakespearean group in England." He chuckled a little. "You may have noticed my English accent." He looked at them expectantly; all nodded. "I rather enjoyed the way they talked and after several years of living in England, acting and all, it just became ingrained in my speech patterns. Oh, I almost forgot. I worked in a museum for a short while in the States, as well."

Continuing on, he said, "I lived in England until around the year 2000 when I returned to the eastern coast of the United States and remarried. Oh, I'm sorry, I forgot to mention that I had married twice while in England to wonderful women, who both passed away." Eyebrows raised in the room. "In 2000, when I arrived in Boston, I met a beautiful lady, who was the light of my life. We married and expected to live happily ever after. While living in Massachusetts I became a masshole, as people there sometimes call themselves." Again, there was a collective raising of eyebrows. "Unfortunately it didn't work out acceptably for either one of us, so we divorced, and I moved back here in 2007 to live the life you see before you."

A brief silence played out until Derrick Hansen nodded to the others. "Mr. Hodges, we thank you very much for your time. I think you have given us some information to chew over and check out."

As he stood up to leave, Rue Shanahan asked, "Oh, one more thing, is recycling aluminum cans your sole means of support?"

"Fortunately, my first two wives were fairly well off and left me with enough money to live comfortably, if I am frugal," Hodges answered. "Am I to understand that I am a person of interest in this investigation?" He looked at Sheriff Lewis.

Cooper Lewis responded, "To be completely honest, Mr. Hodges, yes." He tipped his Stetson as he left and the others trailed him out. Hodges followed them to the door, closed it gently and clicked the lock in place. He then returned to the table and rearranged the chairs.

Chapter 9

"It's him," Lisa said loud enough for all of them to hear.

"Should we go to my office and discuss Mr. Hodges?" Derrick Hansen asked.

All quickly agreed. The breezy winter day played havoc with their car doors as they opened them. It was not a lovely, sunny, thirty degree day in the middle of a Minnesota winter; it was cloudy, windy, and cold. The temperature hovered in the teens and the wind made it feel considerably colder.

Within three minutes they arrived at Chief Hansen's Rose Creek office and were offered coffee by the lone secretary/dispatcher. Lisa gratefully cupped her frozen hands around her warm mug and took the chair nearest Derrick Hansen. Cooper Lewis sat next to her and the other two completed the ring around the table.

"He's our man," Lisa repeated.

"A little early to say, but he definitely strikes me as someone who could have done it. He didn't seem too keen on revealing his past, but he didn't try to sugar coat anything, either," Rue Shanahan commented.

"Is it just me, but did he seem a little odd?" Cooper Lewis asked. Derrick Hansen rested his cup on the table and responded.

"The guy has been here for seven years and I've barely heard a peep out of him. I've only talked to him a couple of times, but I would agree he's...a little eccentric. This was the most I heard him talk in all the time he's been here." He paused while he took a sip from his cup.

―――

"Once in a while we'll get a complaint from someone that he's stalking around their house or business, but he's just looking for cans, or seems to be. As far as his past, I know a little. He grew up here and some of the older people remember him as a kid. His father was a flirt and rumored to have had a few affairs in town, but I don't know of one woman who ever admitted they had a fling with him."

"He's our man. I'd stake my reputation on it," Lisa repeated, but this time more emphatically.

"What makes you so sure?" Shanahan prodded.

"His whole story stinks. I'll bet he's a lecher, like his old man was, because the apple doesn't fall far from the tree. That night, he followed Laura home and tried something when she was drunk. Things didn't go as he planned so he killed her." "Who said she was drunk?" Hansen asked.

"It's in the coroner's report. Her blood alcohol level was beyond .08," Lisa reminded him.

"Come on, try something in the middle of winter on the sidewalk? For Christ's sakes!" Shanahan said. "If I was going to try something of the nature you're suggesting, I'd wait until she got back to her house where it was warm. Hodges seems like the type that would play it a little smarter than you're suggesting, Lisa."

Dolcheski bit her lip and didn't say anything.

Shanahan continued, "Someone intended to kill Laura Walters from the get-go. There wasn't going to be any rape or whatever. The question is why, and I just can't formulate a reason, right now anyway, as to why Gerald Hodges would stalk and kill Laura Walters. I'm not ruling him out, but I think we should do our due diligence and investigate his past. Let's check and see if he has a record in the U.S. or England. And while we're at it, let's check out his Merchant Marine record, too."

"I tend to agree with you, Rue. Let's get our teams of people on this and do some research," Lewis said. Lisa subtly poked Lewis in the ribs and gave him the look, as if to say, "Your team of people is me, and you know it." Chief Hansen's office was as limited as Lewis' was. The only person at the table who had a real team to rely upon was Rue Shanahan. Austin wasn't a thriving metropolis, but with a population standing around twenty-four thousand, it did warrant a larger police department than the surrounding communities.

The others agreed when Rue Shanahan reiterated his feelings about not dismissing Cadence Pieson as a suspect.

Before they departed, they divvied up responsibilities, with the understanding that each department was free to pursue all avenues of investigation if the evidence warranted it. The main rule was to keep in touch and share. Sheriff Lewis was given the responsibility of contacting Beth Reddy and Damien George, and keeping them on a short leash.

Chapter 10

Galena Mendez's husband, Nathan, was out of town this evening and she was home alone enjoying a full-bodied glass of cabernet. She took a sip, let it flow around her back molars, held it for several seconds, and then swallowed. Oh, that was so good, she thought to herself. A glass of wine, or two, or three, every evening, keeps the doctor away. Galena chuckled as she reclined in her favorite spot on the sofa in the walkout basement living room, watching a Monty Python movie she had rented earlier in the day.

She was comfortable and getting more so by the minute. What the hell, I may finish the bottle tonight.

The figure lurking outside the sliding glass door of the walkout could see through the narrow opening of the pulled drapes. She tried the door and smiled when she found it was unlocked. Galena's laughter was easily heard over the turned-up volume of the movie. The door slid noiselessly open on its well-lubricated wheels.

Parting the drapes with one hand while holding a nightstick with the other, she entered the room. The back of Galena's head and shoulders were bobbing up and down while rolls of laughter escaped her.

The figure approached Galena as if she were stalking a deer in the woods. The carpet and subfloor were nearly new, so no creaking accompanied her steps as she proceeded closer. Excitement gripped her as she raised the stick in her right hand and delivered the first blow to the side of Galena's head. A subdued 'thunk' was the only sound heard as Galena blacked out immediately, a fortunate event for sure, as several more blows followed the first, laying waste to her skull and brain.

Trembling, she switched hands holding the nightstick and stretched her right hand to Galena's neck to feel for a pulse. When none was found she turned the body with her gloved hand and felt the other side. Standing straight up on shaky legs and smiling triumphantly, she said to no one, "All done." Her breathing was labored and her hands still shook. Excitement, fear, and a sudden lack of energy filled her as she left the way she had entered, taking care not to leave any signs of her presence.

While walking quickly down the embankment towards the frozen creek, she tripped and fell, sliding several feet. She rose with difficulty, hobbled across the frozen creek, and half walked, half limped, the quarter mile to where she had parked on a short gravel in-drive. There were no houses near the in-drive, which was nearly hidden by oak trees lining its sides. Before opening her car door and spilling light into the night, she swiveled her head in all directions, searching for any signs of life. Seeing none, she quickly entered the car and dropped herself into the driver's seat, quietly closing the door. She worried for several seconds until the overhead light went off. Sitting for another minute, while continuing to check for the presence of anyone near that could discover her, she waited. Nothing moved and no one appeared. No lights on nearby houses came on as her breathing returned to normal.

After starting the vehicle, she slowly backed out of the short driveway and began her journey home, keeping the headlights off until turning onto the main road.

Chapter 11

The news caused a sensation in the surrounding area the next day. A second murder within days of the first shocked everyone, including law enforcement personnel.

Rue Shanahan had hurried to the scene as swiftly as he could the morning of the discovery. A sickening feeling overcame him as he surveyed the victim and the blood splattered sofa. Galina Mendez's vacant eyes stared at the wall paintings on the other side of the room. One arm was twisted underneath her body while the other hung over the edge of the sofa.

"Not very pretty, is it?" one of the detectives on the scene said to Shanahan.

Shanahan shook his head and answered, "No. No it isn't."

"It looks like the killer entered from the sliding glass doors behind the couch over there," the detective offered. He then backed off a little when he sensed that Shanahan had some connection to the victim. Shanahan stood with his hands deep inside his pants pockets for a while and then began looking around the room.

His eyes gravitated to a painting hanging on the wall to the left of the sixty inch flat screen TV. It presented an idyllic scene of a young herdsman of goats in the Tuscan countryside. The colors were vivid and the picture so relaxing that he found it almost impossible to tear his vision away from it, but he did.

He nearly bumped into Derrick Hanson as he turned around. Hanson reflexively stepped back abruptly and shook his head.

"Sorry, Rue. Sometimes I sneak up on people without trying. It's a curse on me that started when I was in Boy Scouts earning my merit badges. The other kids called me Chief Stalking Bear," Derrick Hanson said.

"Now you're just Chief of Police," Shanahan replied.

"Galena Mendez, another member of the book club," Sheriff Lewis said morosely. He towered over them as he stepped closer to the other two. "This is beginning to resemble the modus operandi of a serial killer," he added. The Stetson on top of his head added another four or five inches to his six-foot-nine frame, making the other two appear much smaller than they actually were.

"At first glance this would appear to make Cadence Pieson a stronger suspect than she really is," Shanahan volunteered. Derrick Hanson frowned and Lewis looked at him skeptically. "However, if anything, this makes me want to eliminate her as a suspect. Why would she be so stupid as to come back here and kill the only other person that she tried to shake down?"

"Shake down is the wrong term to use, Rue. Let's not make it something it wasn't," Lewis countered.

"I'd agree it wasn't a shakedown," Hanson said. "More like the act of a beggar. She needed money, and they didn't give it to her, so she kills them? I don't buy that at all. They've all known each other for years so no matter what, the animosity wasn't there, at least not enough of it to make her deliberately kill either victim. And these were deliberate killings. No crimes of passion here."

"I suggest that we spread this out and interview the other members of the book club again. Maybe one or two of them can shed a little more light on the relationships between Pieson, Walters, and Mendez, Maybe there's more to this than we've been lead to believe," Sheriff Cooper Lewis said.

As they walked out of the house together, Shanahan watched the technicians dust for prints and remembered the party he had attended here just a month ago. It had been a well-attended affair with several of the town's elite citizens present, including the mayor, and the CEO of Hormel, the main employer in town.

The Mendez's were good people, and now he was going to have to tell Nathan Mendez that his wife had been murdered. This was not a part of the job he had ever experienced, but now he was going to retreat to his office and call Nathan Mendez. It wasn't a moment he relished.

Hanson and Sheriff Lewis coordinated a statement for the press and then set about divvying up book club members for another round of interviews. Lewis also called Beth Reddy and notified her of Galena's murder. They decided to meet again at six in Rue Shanahan's office.

Beth grabbed her cell phone while running her credit card through the reader in the grocery store and paid the checker as she finished talking to Sheriff Lewis. She picked up her cloth bags filled with groceries and raced to her vehicle in the Hy Vee parking lot. Once she was settled, Beth called Damian, who was at home googling anything he could find about Gerald Hodges.

Damian took the news hard. He hadn't paid attention to any of the local news outlets, so hadn't heard about Galena's murder until now. Beth said she'd be home in half an hour and they would plot the next thread of the investigation.

Thirty-five minutes later she pulled into their garage, unloaded the groceries, and both of them looked at the information Damian had pulled up about Gerald Hodges, virtually nothing besides a 2001 marriage announcement to Lucille Amberworth in the Pickwith Globe, one of the major newspapers in Boston.

The announcement described his recent immigration from England and her Boston pedigree. Her mother was a member of the Daughters of the Revolution and her father was a retired attorney in Boston. A small divorce announcement was also found. The newspaper was dated January 6, 2007.

"Looks like he beat a hasty retreat out of town. Maybe we should contact his former wife and delve into Hodges' past," Damien suggested. "We could get lucky and she'll provides us with some useful information regarding her former husband."

"It's worth a try," Beth agreed.

"I found an address and phone number for her while you were out shopping."

"What are you waiting for? Give her a call."

"You got it," Damien said as he dialed Lucile Amberworth's listed phone number.

"Apparently, she reverted to her maiden name after the divorce."

"Maybe because she really didn't want anyone to know she had been married to Mr. Hodges," Beth posed.

"Or, maybe she's just a liberated woman who never took his name in the first place, or she's a liberated woman who decided to revert to her old name because she couldn't stand the thought of keeping the name of a man she couldn't bear to live with."

"Just look at the marriage announcement again," Beth said, the irritation obvious in her voice.

"Hmm, 'Mr. and Mrs. Gerald Hodges.' Looks like she reverted. I'll bet she couldn't stand the guy."

"How'd she stay married to him for six years?"

"Five and a half; they were married in July, 2001," Damien corrected.

"Call and we'll put her on speaker phone."

Damien dialed the number listed and they waited for an answer. Three rings into the call, an automated voice message told them the number no longer existed. "Well, that's about what I expected," said Damien with a frown. "Nothing can ever be easy in this business."

"Google that free trace phone number site," Beth suggested. As soon as Damien typed in free trace a window appeared where they entered Lucille Amberworth's name and the last city they knew she had resided in, Boston. Magically, her name and address appeared with the last four digits of the phone number blocked out. A small pop-up appeared in the window indicating the number would cost them

"It'll cost us ninety-five cents to get her number. Some free service," Damien said.

"Well, do it. Ninety-five cents isn't going to kill us." He clicked on the pop-up and another window appeared asking for credit card information. He entered their Capitol One account number and clicked again. Lucille's number, including area code appeared.

"Okay, here we go," Damien said as he punched the number into his cell. After three rings, a cultured male voice answered.

Damien began, "Hello. My name is Damien George and I'm trying to contact Lucille Amberworth. Is she in?"

There was a pause on the other end and a muffled voice could be heard as if the person holding the phone had held his hand over the receiver while talking to someone else. "What is the nature of your call?" the male voice asked.

"The call concerns Ms. Amberworth's former husband, Gerald Hodges, and some events that have occurred in Minnesota where he lives." Damien and Beth could hear the jostle of the phone as it changed hands and an anxious female voice spoke.

"Did something happen to Gerald? Please tell me."

"Are we speaking to Lucille Amberworth?" Beth cut in.

"Yes, you are. I thought I was speaking to a Damien George."

"I'm sorry, we're on a speaker phone. My name is Elizabeth Reddy and my associate, Damien George, called you. Nothing has happened to Gerald Hodges, but he is a person of interest in a double murder investigation and we thought you may be able to answer a few background questions to assist us in the investigation."

"Oh, my God!" Lucille said. "Are you the police?"

"No, we are private investigators hired by friends of the victims and are assisting the police as they try to solve the crimes. You could be of great service to the authorities by answering a few questions."

Sounding a bit annoyed, Lucille replied, "I'm sorry, but I'm not going to answer any questions over the phone like this. For all I know this may be a cruel prank."

"We understand your concern, Ms. Amberworth. We'll contact our local police and arrange for them to get ahold of the authorities in Boston so they may interview you regarding this matter," Beth responded sympathetically.

Before she hung up, Lucille softened slightly and asked, "Is Gerald in jail?"

"No, but as I said, he is a person of interest in this investigation and the authorities would like to visit his background and get a more complete picture of him. He is not very well known in the area and more information could help put any further questions concerning his possible involvement in the murders to rest." A sigh could be heard on the other end of the phone and it was clear Lucille was hesitating while considering sustaining the conversation. Damien and Beth waited to see if she said anything more.

Suddenly she asked, "Do you have a Mac?"

"What do you mean?" Beth asked.

"I mean do you have an Apple computer?"

Damien jumped in, "Yes, we do. Why do you ask?"

"Does your computer have the latest version of operating software?"

"Yes, yes," Damien answered.

"I will talk to you, but I want to see your faces. I can tell a lot by seeing who I am speaking to. I want to FaceTime you. Give me your name again and your email address. Here is mine." She recited her full name and email address. "Now put me into your address book and I'll do the same with you. I'll call you within five minutes."

They did as she said and waited. Within a few minutes FaceTime came alive with a call from Lucille Amberworth. Damien clicked the green telephone icon and soon they were face-to-face with an older, pretty woman, with full gray hair and streaks of blond highlights. A little taken aback that Gerald Hodges could have been married to the attractive woman before them, Damien actually popped his head up and backward a notch. Beth was more composed.

"Ah, that's better," Ms. Amberworth said as she appeared to study their faces. "Please stand up and turn around." They both did as they had been politely commanded. "All right, now, if your computer is a laptop, pan around your office, house, or whatever it is, and show me any proof that says you are who you say you are and that, indeed, you are private investigators."

They both retrieved their licenses and brought them up close to the camera so Lucille could read them. Beth panned the camera on the computer around the office so she could view the two Minnesota P.I. certificates hanging on the wall, lingering there until Amberworth said okay.

"I want to see the license plate on your car," Lucille said. Damien carried the computer to the attached garage and focused on the plate, and then he opened the garage door to reveal the snow-filled landscape enveloping Stewartville, Minnesota.

"Okay, I'll answer your questions," Amberworth finally said. And then she changed her mind. "I want to see a newspaper article that corroborates what you've told me about the crime." Moving swiftly to an end table, Beth fetched the issue of the Rochester Post Bulletin that dealt with the first murder and held the headline story about Laura Walters' murder in front of the isight camera on their MacBook.

"Please enlarge it." Beth held it closer as Ms. Amberworth wrote down the name of the article, newspaper, and date. "There, I'll google this later."

"A second murder occurred just last night and will probably be in today's newspaper, so you may want to google that as well." Damien suggested.

"Thank you. That is exactly what I will do," Amberworth replied. "Now, please ask your questions."

"First of all, do you have any objections to us recording this interview?"

"Of course not," Amberworth replied.

"Were you married to Gerald Hodges in 2001?" Damien asked.

"Yes, we were married on July 12, 2001, in St. Patrick's Cathedral."

"And you divorced in 2006?"

"Actually, 2007," Amberworth corrected. "And then he moved to Minnesota. We've kept in periodic contact until about a year ago, when he no longer wrote or telephoned me. Nor did he answer my correspondences."

"So you were on pretty good terms with Mr. Hodges after the divorce?"

"We loved each other. It wasn't hard to remain fond of one another. I wanted to stay in touch with him, and I thought that was his wish...at least until the past year. I don't know what changed. I care

for Gerald deeply and retain only kind and loving thoughts of him."
Beth and Damien exchanged cross-eyed looks.

"Ms. Amberworth, given your expressed thoughts that you still care
and love Mr. Hodges, could you please tell us what precipitated the
divorce?" Beth asked. Ms. Amberworth paused and stared down at her
feet. Only the top of her head, revealing thinning hair and a small bald
spot was visible to Damien and Beth. A tiny hiccup-like cry escaped
from Amberworth's lips.

"Gerald is a very special man who presents special challenges to
anyone who chooses to become close to him." She raised her face to
the camera and a wistful, faraway look filled the lens. "Although he is
a wonderful, romantic man, whom I adored from the very first
moment I met him at one of the governor's open houses, Gerald can
be maddeningly precise and argumentative about the smallest issues
that commonly arise between two people who are living together.
Those issues ultimately led to the realization to both of us that we
couldn't continue to live together and still be friends. We still loved
each other, but we came to a civilized, mutual decision that we would
divorce. Gerald decided to carry it a step further and moved to
Minnesota after his mother died to reside in her house. Personally, I
just think it was too painful for him to live in Boston and be reminded
every day, through newspaper articles, television, and whatever, that I
was carrying on an active life that brought me into daily contact with
other men. Whether I like it or not, I belong to a prominent Boston
family and I have social responsibilities that I have to fulfill.

"It hurt Gerald to see me out in the company of other people,
especially men, even though I told him they were only friends."

Amberworth stopped and collected her thoughts, giving Beth a chance to ask another question.

"Ms. Amberworth, Gerald Hodges has been what you would call a character in Rose Creek, the town he lives in now. So we see why you would call him special, because he is obviously different than anyone we've ever met. He is a person of interest in the investigation because of his habit of spying on-no, I'll change that, intensely observing-other people, especially women within Rose Creek." Amberworth appeared uncomfortable. "Is there anything else about Mr. Hodges you can tell us that may help explain his 'interest' in other women?"

The uncomfortable look remained on Amberworth's face as she nervously looked from one side to the other, obviously contemplating what to say. "I think Gerald needs help, counseling, something that will help him overcome his need to, to... I just don't know if this is helpful to mention this or not. I don't know why I'm confiding this to you over the Internet like this, but you two seem sincere and, damn it, I guess it's going to come out sooner or later. Gerald is a transvestite! I think his interest in women is because he studies them, their movements, fashions, the way they walk and talk. I think he uses them so, when he dresses up, he can look and feel more like a woman. There, I said it! I've been wanting to say it out loud for years, and now I've done it.

"He is such an enigma, what with his perfectionism, lining things up perfectly, beginning each day the same way, folding towels, etc., etc. It never quits and it wears on anyone that is around him for any length of time." She sighed. "And then, on the other hand, he is extremely romantic and would provide the most beautiful settings for dining, and when he made love, it was…" Her voice trailed off as she caught herself providing too much information. "In the end, you add it all up and I couldn't take it, and he knew it, so we divorced. That was that."

Mesmerized, Damien and Beth were caught off guard and said nothing for several moments. Finally, Beth spoke. Ms. Amberworth, you have been very helpful. We want you to know that we will forward the recording of this interview to our local law enforcement officers and they will be contacting you in the very near future. We're sure they will have more questions and will want to talk with you personally. Do you have any questions or requests for us at this time?"

Amberworth looked pensive. "When you see Gerald again, please keep in mind the private comments I have shared with you. He is a wonderful man who needs sympathetic ears. And I am assuming that none of the details concerning Gerald's…condition will be shared with the media. He doesn't deserve the ridicule and negative attention."

There was another pause. "I can only assure you that none of this will come to light if Mr. Hodges has had nothing to do with the murders that have occurred," Beth said.

Lucille started to say something but changed her mind and simply nodded her head. Damien briefly summarized the interview and asked if she agreed with what he had said. Amberworth said yes. Beth thanked Ms. Amberworth and then terminated the Internet connection.

"I wonder if any of this is going to help us at all," Damien wondered aloud.

"Well, you never know, but I think we need to pay a little clandestine visit to Mr. Hodges sometime soon," Beth said.

Damien looked confused as he turned towards her. "Why? So he's a cross-dresser and a little Aspergerish. I don't see why that makes him any more worthy of a clandestine visit than anyone else on her list, including Cadence Pieson. Come to think of it, she is the only other one on our list right now. And, you do know that breaking and entering is a crime and that any evidence we would gain from such an act could not be used in a court of law?"

"Of course I realize that, but I don't think we would need to break and enter. I think he just might leave his house open for anyone to walk into." She said it with a wink.

"No, no, no, no, no, we're not gonna do anything like that."

"It seems like at one time, you told me you're the boss."

"Wait a second, I said that you were the lead person and I…would…follow. Okay, you made your point. When do you want to do this?"

"Let's find out when he has his meetings with his guy friends at the municipal. Then you go down, observe him while I check around his place. We both have phones, so you call me when he is leaving and I get out and come pick you up. No one is the wiser, and just maybe I find something that helps us in this case."

Shaking his head, Damien said, "I don't really like that at all, but…you're the boss and we'll do what you want."

She smiled as she said, "That's the spirit! I knew you would see the light and agree."

"Oh, one more thing, if everything is locked up and you can't let yourself in?" Damien asked.

"You know I have skills in this area," Beth said emphatically.

"Yeah, I know. For now, I'd better prepare this recording and forward it to Shanahan, Chief Hanson, and Sheriff Lewis." As Damien worked on the computer, Beth made phone calls to each law enforcement office, letting them know who they had been able to contact and alerting them that the video of the interview they had just finished would soon arrive in their email boxes.

To her surprise it was Cooper Lewis who picked up the phone at the Spirit Grove Law Enforcement Office. "Great job, Beth, I'll let you know what we find out about Gerald Hodges' life in the Merchant Marine and his years in the Shakespearean company in England," Sheriff Lewis told her.

She thanked him but didn't mention her plan to enter Gerald Hodges' home and look for any damning evidence she could find.

Chapter 12

The evening was beautiful. Large snowflakes were floating lazily down from the darkened sky and settling onto the windshield she peered through, making it difficult to see clearly. An occasional flick of her wrist moved the wand and the wipers removed the built-up snow, allowing her to keep her vigil in front of Claude's apartment house.

She had been watching for a couple of hours now and had not seen her target enter the building. Maybe the target wouldn't show up tonight, but she hoped she would.

Staking out any place had never been a chore for her and tonight wasn't any different. There was always something to occupy her mind, whether it be an invented game, such as the one now, where she would count the number of seconds between wiper swipes on the windshield

Sometimes the weather conditions would jog a long-lost memory of her childhood, like tonight. The memory was not a pleasant one, however. Her hands tightly gripped the steering wheel as tears leaked from the corners of her eyes. Mascara trickled down her cheeks while the memory continued its course.

It was Christmas Eve. She had been twelve years old and, as now, snow was falling. Happy times were being enjoyed by her broken little family when her mother obtained a new job at the hospital. Since her father had been attending regular Alcoholics Anonymous meetings for the past five months, he was handling life better. He hadn't taken a drink or hit her mother or her during that time. Life was as glorious as she had ever remembered it and she was distinctly happy and grateful.

The snow had been falling softly while she and her mother strolled the sidewalks and peeked in the store front windows, laughing, pointing, even skipping, until nearly slipping on the light, fresh snow. They hadn't the money to buy new coats, mittens, scarves, or anything like that, but neither of them cared. They were happy and a better future could be seen.

Stopping in for spiced, hot cider at Ladford's Bakery was all they could hope for this Christmas Eve, so they did. It was glorious. She could never remember anything tasting so good as the sweet, hot cider as the snow fell around them. It nearly took her breath away as she cupped it in her old, yellow mittens while her mother entwined one of her arms around hers and they walked home.

As soon as they stepped inside the door of the small, two-bedroom bungalow, she and her mother knew something was wrong. The artificial Christmas tree had been knocked over and ornaments were strewn over the living room floor. The tree lights had been pulled from the wall plug, destroying the intended festive mood of the evening.

The two of them just stood silently, tightening the grips they had on each other's hand. A few seconds passed before they heard her father yelling for her mother to come to their bedroom immediately. Their eyes met and she could see the fear in her mother. She was also afraid. Every good feeling they had just experienced left them as if a great vacuum had been created in the house and sucked it away.

He called for her again, "Damn it, Marie, get in here now!" Her mother let go of her hand and haltingly walked the twenty steps or so to their bedroom.

"I'm coming, Gus." She tried to say it cheerfully, but it sounded more like she was taking her last walk to the death chamber.

The little girl that she was back then was frozen in the open doorway. Realizing that the cold air was beginning to envelope her, she shivered, shut the door behind her, and then stood and waited. Soon, it came. The crack of a hard slap against her mother's cheek reverberated throughout the house. She wet her pants as she stood paralyzed.

Another slap and she then heard her father's angry voice. "I need you to get me another bottle now!" Her mother cried and protested that she couldn't leave their daughter in the house. "Take her with you then, damn it! Just get it and hurry back."

Her mother came sobbing out of the bedroom. The mark on her cheek was red and throbbing. Her mother clutched the ten-dollar bill he had thrown at her to buy his favorite Kentucky Bourbon.

Recovering slightly, her mother said, "Come along. We've got to go to the store."

"Mom, I can't. I wet my pants," she cried.

"We just have to go now." Her mother grabbed her hand and pulled her out of the house to which they never returned.

When the memory faded, she found herself gripping the steering wheel even more tightly than before. Picking up a Kleenex tissue, she roughly swabbed her eyes and cheeks. She then checked her watch. God, it had been seven minutes since she had been aware of anything happening in the outside world. Frantically, she looked around the area and noticed a red auto had parked near Claude's car in one of the spaces in front of the apartment house.

She smiled as little gurgles of cries escaped her. Cadence must be here.

Chapter 13

It was Monday and Damien had found out that Gerald Hodges and his sometime buddies always met at the municipal at seven p.m. The plan was set. They would drive to Rose Creek where Beth would drop Damien off at the muni to keep track of Mr. Hodges while she took a short road trip to Hodges' house and looked for anything out of the ordinary inside. That seemed like a given, knowing the subject and all of his known idiosyncrasies.

Snow was falling softly as Damien left the car and entered the municipal. There was a nice crowd in the little place so he got a Diet Coke from the tall drink of water behind the bar and tried to slide, unnoticed, over to a small table away from the one Hodges and his cronies occupied in the far corner. Boston Whitley noticed Damien enter the bar almost immediately

"Hey," he said to his friends at the table. "Junior just came in." The others cast their eyes to where Boston was looking.

"Well, well, well. I think it is," said Earl Mancoat. "I'll bet we can expect Miss Beautiful to come in any second."

"She's probably parking the car. Jesus, I'll bet he makes her drive the damn car everywhere."

"Yeah, like a little chauffeur," Seth Tryton added sneeringly.

"It's plain to see who the brains of that outfit is," huffed Mancoat, as Gerald Hodges sat silently. Mancoat continued, "I got an idea, let's invite Junior over and we'll pump him for information."

Hodges perked up, "Capital idea," he said.

Mancoat rose and hobbled over to Damien's small, high-top table. "Junior, come on over and join us. We're having good 'man' conversations over there, and we figure you might learn something." Damien, who had been watching Mancoat cross the bar to his table, didn't answer right away and frowned.

Eyebrows raised, Mancoat tried again. "What's the matter, too much testosterone for a young buck like yourself? Come on, have a beer, er, uh, or a Diet Coke, and let us know what's happening with your investigation." Mancoat sneaked a peak at his compatriots at the other table and winked.

Gathering momentum to rise up and join the party, Damien rose stood and said, "Okay, I'll be with you in a second. Gotta go to the bathroom first."

Mancoat smiled a widely, "Great, kid! Take a piss and come on over. I'll bring your Coke." He picked up the drink and limped back over to the old mens' table while Damien took his time walking over to the bathroom. He entered, waited until the gentleman ahead of him had left after using the facilities, and then took out his cell phone and texted Beth that he was joining the old guys. He finished, washed his hands out of habit, and went back to sit with the old guys.

As Damien sat down in a chair that had been pulled out for him by Seth Tryton, Gerald Hodges extended his hand. Damien grasped it and was surprised by the strength of Hodges' grip.

"So good to see you, old boy," Hodges stated in his acquired English accent.

"It's good to see you as well, Mr. Hodges."

"Call me Gerald please or better yet, Gerry. That's what they all call me here."

The others chimed in. "That's right, Gerry," they said in unison while staring at Damien, making him distinctly uncomfortable. Shifting in his chair, he wondered if the little group had an ulterior motive for asking him to join them.

"So, Damien, if I may call you that, could you share any tidbits of your investigation with us?" Hodges asked.

"Actually, there isn't much to share at this point. As you know, the police have some persons of interest they are doing some background work on." He delivered the words while staring at Hodges. The others, except for Hodges, shook their heads no. Hodges smiled a half smile and concurred.

He looked at his fellow old men. "I regret that I did not inform my friends I have been told I am one of those persons of interest," he said.

His "friends" were all silent for a moment until Earl Mancoat spoke up. "Ha, good one, Gerry. Why would they think a harmless old guy like yourself, hell like any of us here, could be involved in a murder?"

"He's not joking, uh, I'm sorry, I forgot your name," Damien said to Mancoat.

"Mancoat, Earl," he said forcefully.

"I'm sorry, Mr. Mancoat, but he's not joking. The authorities think that Gerry might know more than he's told them so far."

"And what do you think, Junior?" Boston Whitley asked.

"Me? I tend to leave the thinking up to my boss."

"Ah yes, Miss Reddy. Speaking of her, where is she tonight?" Hodges asked.

Damien, who was not prepared to be interrogated by the person he was supposed to keep an eye on tonight, struggled to answer the question.

After dropping Damien off at the muni, Beth drove to Gerald Hodges' house. She made sure the volume was turned up on her cell phone so she could hear Damien's incoming call, alerting her that Hodges was leaving the bar and she would have only a few minutes before he arrived home and discovered her searching his house.

She walked boldly to his door and knocked for the benefit of any neighbors who might be watching. After waiting several moments and keeping a watchful eye, Beth took out her tools and opened the door. Quickly, she entered and closed it behind her.

The dining room was exactly as she remembered it from their interview with Hodges a few days before. Chairs were spaced neatly on both sides and ends of the table and she marveled at the lack of change in anything she could observe within the kitchen.

Working as efficiently as she knew how, Beth moved through each room in the house, opening doors, drawers, and looking behind cabinets. After moving anything, she took care to return it to its rightful place.

Opening his bedroom closet and looking inside, she was slightly surprised when she found only men's clothing. The same surprised attitude befell her as she opened dresser drawers and found only the what you would normally expect.

Descending to the basement, Beth found it easy to survey the contents that were all neatly arranged around a partially finished area on the right-hand side. Again, as she inspected everything observable, nothing out of the ordinary could be seen. It wasn't until she walked upon the far end of the concrete floor that she felt something that peaked her suspicions. The floor had a distinctly different sound as she walked over it, and yet, it appeared to be no different than the rest of the concrete covering.

Feeling like a little kid, Beth jumped around the area and established a perimeter outlining a rectangular area. She strained to see a break in the concrete. Needing more light, she remembered a flashlight stashed in a cabinet upstairs. Beth leaped the stairs two at a time and retrieved it. As she returned to the basement, her cell rang and, recognizing the ring tone as Damien's, she picked up immediately.

"Get out of there now, he's coming!" She hesitated; she really wanted to find out about the space she had discovered, but, reluctantly, Beth ran upstairs, returned the flashlight to its spot, turned off the lights, locked the door, and ran to her car. She took the long way around the little town so that she wouldn't take the chance of Gerald Hodges seeing her car near his home.

Damien was anxiously watching from the doorway of the municipal and walked out to meet her as she pulled into the parking lot.

"Did you get inside without any problems?" Damien asked immediately.

"No problems, I used a few tricks Bennie had taught me and opened the place right up. And I don't think he'll be any the wiser for it." Not able to contain her excitement, Beth revealed what she had found in the basement. Uncharacteristically, she let her imagination run wild. "I think it may be a hidden room below the basement. The entire floor looks like it's covered with concrete, but it's definitely got a different, hollow sound when you walk on one part of it. I wanted to get a look at it with better light, but that's when you called and I had to get out of there. We've got to get back in there and find out what the hell it is."

"You know for once, I guess twice now, I'm ready to go along with you on something I normally wouldn't."

She cleared off the windshield to get another unobstructed view of the car. For sure, it was Cadence Pieson's. When she slammed her fist onto the dash, it caused a hairline fracture to appear in the gray matte. Rage began to boil inside of her. How dare Cadence do this? Claude was hers.

She would wait for fifteen more minutes. If Cadence didn't come out, she would go in. She knew Claude had changed the locks to his apartment, but that would not be a problem for her. She could enter and exit anytime she wanted. Her rage began to actually soothe her pain at feeling betrayed. An uncanny, irrational calmness overcame her as she formulated a plan that brought a sliver of a smile to her face.

Several minutes later, wearing thin gloves, she exited her vehicle and entered the apartment building by punching in the security numbers. He may have changed his apartment locks, but he couldn't do anything about the entrance to the building, she thought. A security camera stared her in the face, but she was not worried. Taking the steps by twos, she made it to the third floor in no time. She could find her way to his room blindfolded and falling down drunk if she had to. She didn't have to.

Stopping in front of apartment 318, she listened for a few minutes. Hearing nothing, she opened the door without trouble and entered a darkened room. The bedroom door was closed and she could hear the moans coming from Cadence. Her face, flushed red with anger as she moved to the thermostat, turned it up as high as it would go, and waited. Ten, twenty, forty minutes passed and the room was becoming uncomfortably hot. She removed her clothes and stole silently to the bedroom door. Claude and Cadence were speaking in low voices, mumbling words she couldn't make out, but she could recognize fear in the tones. She smiled. Good!

Claude was beginning to rise from the bed when she entered. He froze when he saw her naked, silhouetted figure. Cadence gasped as she pulled the sheets around her neck.

"Kristen, please, I don't want trouble," Claude said shakily as he rose a little further off the bed.

"Can you feel the heat?" she asked. "You know it's the way I like it, don't you," she said to Claude. "And Cadence, how do you like it? Does it make you feel all warm and fuzzy inside? I know it must on the outside because I can smell your sweat."

A hint of recognition dented Cadence; she knew this person, she was sure of it. Where, where, had she met her? Her mind raced to retrieve the missing information of where they had met and the identity of the person who threatened both her and Claude.

She moved around the edge of the bed while the two of them seemed to be frozen in time. Sensing a strike from the nightstick the naked figure wielded, Claude moved as quickly as he could to intercept the anticipated blow. She was faster and the blow smashed his curled arm, breaking it. Claude yelled in pain as another blow cracked him in the same place. Howling, he didn't notice Cadence get up and run for the door. Again, she was faster and delivered a crushing blow to Cadences' back, sending her to the floor, mouthing cries that no one heard.

As Cadence lay sprawled on her stomach, gasping for air, another blow smashed into the back of her skull, killing her instantly. Claude's scream for help was cut off by another blow. This one to his cheekbone, turning it into an amalgam of crushed bone and loosened teeth floating around inside of his mouth. His vision was hazy until several more blows to the head finished the job and he lay lifeless.

After arranging the bodies, she stood triumphantly, breathing easily. She hadn't broken a sweat, and, except for the blood covering her body, there was not a mark on her. She was careful to touch nothing, although she still wore the latex gloves. Walking briskly to the bathroom, she literally jumped inside the shower and washed every drop of blood down the drain. She wiped down the walls with the squeegee hanging from a suction cup holder. Satisfied that not a trace of her remained anywhere, she dressed in the outer room and turned the heat down as low as it would go. She reasoned that maybe the bodies would be preserved a while longer in the cooler air and discovery of them would take longer.

After surveying the carnage she had wrought, she stood for awhile, listening inside the doorway before leaving and making sure no one was in the hallway to see her.

Chapter 14

"I had a slightly tense moment when Hodges asked me where you were this evening. I hadn't quite prepared for that question since I wasn't even supposed to be talking to the guy tonight."

"So what did you tell him?" Beth asked, while carefully negotiating a bend in Highway 56 before it intersected I-90.

"I said that you were talking to one of the old ladies in town, trying to verify some information she had given us a couple of days ago," he answered.

"That was pretty lame. He probably didn't believe it because he'd be wondering, why did Damien George come into this bar while I'm here. Coincidence?"

"I don't know, I think I sounded pretty convincing. I added that I had needed a break and wasn't really looking forward to any HGTV talk or comparing recipes. He acted like he actually understood and sympathized with me." Beth nodded her head, not really believing that Hodges bought the story, but it didn't matter anyway, now.

Hodges said goodbye to the other old coots and waved as he walked out of the municipal and across the highway to the main residential section of town where he lived. The snow had stopped falling now, but the crisp air remained, from which he drew heavy breaths. The walk was no more than three hundred yards to his house and he covered the distance easily using his long strides.

He really enjoyed his visits with the other old men. Sometimes, when the conversation lagged, he would start quoting Shakespeare and the other guys always cracked up. Yes, he enjoyed being with them. In fact, these days he looked upon the meetings as the best times of his life. He actually whistled as he made his way home, still immersed in the good time he had just had. Although, that Damien fellow crept into his mind as he turned the last corner to his house. The young man wasn't as stupid as he appeared; he was certain of that. When asked about the whereabouts of Miss Reddy, he'd hesitated. That may not have been perceptible to the other old men, but it didn't escape Gerald.

He stopped and a smile appeared on his face. My goodness, she paid my house a visit, he thought. Suddenly, his splendid mood returned, his strides lengthened and the tune he whistled became louder. There was now a perkiness to the tune that it had lacked before his enlightenment.

He didn't expect she would still be there, because obviously, Damien George had signaled her he had left the municipal and she should clear out of the house. This was getting him more excited than ever. He was almost giddy as he whistled, sang, and skipped through the snow to his home.

When he stopped in front of the house, he looked for tire and boot tracks. There were too many tire tracks in the street as it was and none in his driveway. Small boot tracks could be seen leading away from the curb and toward his house. He chuckled. His game would begin now. Did she place everything back in its place or did she make a careless mistake? He smiled and chuckled again as he opened the front door, carefully stepped inside and surveyed the kitchen. He took his time as he eyed the outside of every cabinet, the refrigerator, countertop and chair. There was nothing obviously out of place, but he would complete a more detailed inspection of the insides in a moment.

Before he moved from the doorway, however, he gazed at the linoleum floor. Hmmm, no snow, water, or dirt was visible. Must have taken off her boots and left them on the small rug he was standing on. Damn it. I should have looked at the rug before I stepped on it. Now I can't tell if the wet spot on the rug is because of her boots or mine. He cursed himself again for his 'unforced' error, as the tennis announcers called it.

Hodges removed his boots and inspected the refrigerator and then the cupboards. Ah, the flashlight wasn't quite where he had left it. She had been here. A triumphant smile and cackling laugh rose from his bowels. "I knew it, I knew it," he said aloud. The laughter continued as he basked in his powers of thought and observation.

Proceeding to his bedroom and closet area, again, he noticed changes. Pants and shirt hangers had been moved around and left askew. Askew only to him, for no one else would ever have noticed a difference. He moved to the bathroom and opened his medicine cabinet. Nothing was changed there. All over-the-counter medications and his cholesterol pills were exactly where he had left them. He quickly went through the rest of the main floor, keen to any disruptions that may have occurred.

When he was satisfied he had found all the discrepancies upstairs, he descended the steps to the basement. He found no changes, but the thought did occur to him that if he were a messier housekeeper, he would be able to see footprints in the dust on the floor. Well, that thought was only fleeting, because he could never exist in a domain where he had to breathe in filthiness.

He wondered aloud if she had noticed the special door in the basement floor that allowed him to keep his secrets from everyone. He knew, to his dismay that the sound of one's footfalls changed as a person stepped on the hidden doorway he had installed himself several years ago. The sound when stepping on the doorway did not match the rest of the floor. He had tried everything he could think of: more insulation, reinforced wooden perimeter, a collapsing pole that supported the door, but nothing made the sounds uniform across the basement floor.

Gerald had engineered a doorway that fit perfectly with the rest of the concrete flooring. No seam could be seen or felt, even by him. In fact, the only way he could find the edge on the first try was to go to the shelf on the wall opposite the stairs coming from the main floor, measure outwards from the center of the wall precisely four feet, nine and a quarter inches, run his fingers along the floor and feel for it.

Fortunately, he did not have to do that. He had engineered a hydraulic lift system which used a remote control device to open and close the door. Hodges walked to the shelf, noticed that the old jewelry box of his mothers had not been disturbed, opened it and removed the false bottom. He then took out the remote control, pushed the button and watched as the floor rose to reveal the steps entering his most secret compartment.

Taking the remote with him, he walked down and searched his collection of women's clothing and accessories. He passed by the purse he had taken from Cadence Pieson's car several months ago. It contained her driver's license, credit cards, twenty-one dollars worth of cash, a small amount of change, and the mother lode of make-up and moisturizers. His Obsessive Compulsive Disorder compelled him to check everything in his treasure trove of women's things. When he was satisfied nothing had been disturbed, and therefore undiscovered, he breathed a small sigh of relief and returned to the basement.

Gerald closed the hydraulic door, returned the remote to the hiding place within the jewelry box and went upstairs to his living room for a shot of brandy.

"We're going to have to get back in Hodges' basement and find out what the heck is down there. There's something, and I'm not giving up until I find it," Beth said.

"I've gotta admit, you really peaked my curiosity with your discovery, Beth. We would have to distract Hodges for quite a while to give us time to figure out how to get into whatever is there."

"I think I know just the person, or persons who could do it, Carin, Jenny, and maybe Celia Orth. Celia was a debater in high school and is probably the most persuasive person I've ever met. Again, we could set it up so they could warn us when he was about to come back from wherever or whatever they get him involved in." "Well, they've done it before, and I'm sure they would be willing to do it again," Damien said. "I can't believe I'm saying this, but this kind of reminds me of a Nancy Drew mystery. Oh boy!" he groaned.

Beth looked at him and cringed. "I can't believe you said that either." They both took deep breaths and resolved to get ahold of Celia in the morning, enlist her help, and set something up.

Beth was awake long before the alarm woke Damien. She got up, showered and dressed before he was out of bed. As he was getting ready, she phoned Celia, explained what she had found, and asked if she would be willing to "occupy" Gerald Hodges for an extended period of time while she and Damien illegally entered Hodges' home and tried to determine what lay beneath the basement.

Celia was more than willing to take on the duty and said she would contact Jenny and Carin to see if one or both would help her. Fifteen minutes after they had hung up, Beth received a call from Celia saying both Jenny and Carin would help in whatever way they could. Thinking back over the past couple of years, Beth could think of no better friends than Carin, Jenny, and Celia, who at one time or another, had helped her when she needed it most. And now, they were willing to do it again, even though they could be endangering their own lives.

Chapter 15

The bodies were discovered two days later by Claude's sister, who had become concerned when he hadn't answered her phone calls or texts. It just wasn't like him at all, she had told the police. When Ricky Pieson returned home, he reported Cadence missing, although he wasn't sure that she hadn't just run off with someone.

Two Rochester police detectives had been dispatched to the scene. One of them, Bob Caltwell, immediately noticed the similarity to the recent murders in Rose Creek and Austin, and called the office of the Rochester Chief of Police to pass on his suspicions. He, in turn, contacted all the members of the law enforcement team investigating the other two murders. Sheriff Cooper Lewis responded first, and being the closest to Rochester, was at the scene within twenty minutes.

There was something obviously different about this murder, however. The bodies had been rearranged after they had been killed. Great dents in their skulls were readily observable, although blood partially hid the areas that had been bludgeoned.

Lewis stood back and observed the two victims. They had been propped up in bed, their arms tied around each other with a sliced off section of lamp cord. Their eyes stared as their heads rested together.

"The man's name is Claude Peltier" said Detective Caltwell, "and the woman is…" He was cut off in mid-sentence by Lewis.

"Cadence Pieson," Lewis said.

"You know her?" The detective asked.

"She's another member of the Rose Creek and Austin book club that now counts three members killed," Lewis answered. "The gentleman, I don't know."

"It's just my first impression of this crime scene, but it looks to me like there was a little vengeance extracted in this murder. It's almost like the murderer was telling us that this was personal," said Detective Caltwell. "Who bothers to arrange his victims in an embrace? It looks to me like the perp followed her, caught them in bed, and in a jealous rage killed them both."

"Well, I suppose we can ask Richard Pieson about that," Lewis said, apparently agreeing with the detective. "The whole set-up is different than the other two killings, and Richard Pieson would appear to be a reasonable suspect here. It's not like the other two where no one jumps out at you at all, which is so damn puzzling."

"Yeah, it's always the spouse," chimed in Jennings, the other Rochester detective.

"We'll get the technicians in here to dust for prints, but something tells me we're not going to find anything," said Caltwell. "The whole place seems really clean, except for the spatters of blood everywhere in this room." He realized the ridiculousness of what he had said and became silent.

"Wow, the person who did this must have been covered in blood, too. You don't spray that much blood around without getting some on yourself," Jennings offered.

"We'll check the security video footage and see what turns up."

"Got any idea about the time of death?" Lewis asked the forensic pathologist who had been standing silently nearby.

Happy to be consulted, the pathologist said, "Based upon the rigor mortis that has set in, dried blood, and the way blood has congealed around the back of the man and the stomach of the woman, my best guess is between forty-eight and seventy-two hours ago. He died on his back here," he pointed to a pool of blood on the floor, "and she died on her stomach over there," pointing to another small pool of blood on the opposite side of the floor, "and then they were moved to this position in the bed."

Lewis said, "So, whoever moved them had to be fairly strong to muscle them up onto the bed and arrange them in an embrace."

"Bingo," said the pathologist.

"I don't think too many women could muscle a dead body around like that," Caltwell offered.

"I'd agree. Not too many," Lewis said while rubbing the day-old stubble on his chin, thinking back to the time when Lisa Dolcheski had manhandled eighty pound sacks of cement when he helped her mix concrete. Some women, though, can outmuscle most men, he thought.

Rue Shanahan and Derrick Hansen stepped into the room, being careful to avoid the areas marked off by chalk. Soon after, Beth and Damien entered.

"What is this, a circus?" half joked Detective Caltwell.

"Not to worry, detective. I'll introduce you," Lewis said. The detectives from Rochester shook hands with the additional law enforcement personnel and filled them in on everything presently known. Reddy and George stayed silent for the most part, not intending to let anyone in on their planned visitation to Mr. Hodges' home.

Detective Caltwell said that he would be sure to bring the others into the station when the security video from the past few days was available to be viewed.

As Reddy and George left the building, both of them remarked about how this murder definitely looked and felt different from the other two. Richard Pieson was a suspect, since this did look like a vengeful, jealousy-driven murder, but time would tell on that count. Beth couldn't help expressing that this was a hell of a way to get their feet wet in their new business venture. Damien concurred.

Right now they had plans that went beyond Richard Pieson. This was the day where Carin, Jenny, and Celia were going to distract Mr. Hodges while the two of them found out what the hell was under the basement.

Damien, still sensitive of the old men's talk the other evening, when he had been teased about making Beth chauffeur him around, was driving today. He turned off Highway 63 onto I-90W and headed for Austin. Carin, Jenny, and Celia would meet them at Kenny's Oak Grill and go over the plan once more before it was put into action.

The plan called for a meeting with Mr. Hodges and the three ladies. They were to contact him and set up a lunch at Harry's Hash House in Rose Creek, ostensibly to ask him about Cadence and if he knew any other details of her life that would help solve her murder. They were going to approach it purely as friends of the victim who wanted to do everything they could to help the police. The plan called for prolonging the meeting by using lots of flattery for Mr. Hodges and a little flirting if necessary, to prolong the meeting, thus giving Beth and

Damien extra time to open the door Beth had found and discover what was under his basement.

Gerald Hodges learned about the murder of Cadence Pieson while sitting at his breakfast table enjoying a cup of tea and watching the news on his tiny TV set. He gripped the cup tightly in both hands as the News 10 morning reporter began to describe the murders of Cadence Pieson and Claude Peltier. Tears formed and dribbled slowly down his cheeks.

"Cadence," he whispered, as he wiped the salty fluid from his face. He cringed and buried his face in his hands as he heard how the back of her head had been smashed in and her naked body displayed in bed next to Peltier. For several moments after the reporter had finished, Hodges stared at the television, not hearing or seeing what else was reported.

The grief he felt overwhelmed him to the point of paralysis, and he appeared to be in a catatonic state from which he would never awaken. He sat that way, not moving a millimeter from his chair for two hours, until he drew a long, wistful breath and finally stood. He knew what he must do now. Hodges was halfway down the basement stairs when he heard the phone ring. Stopping momentarily, a small measure of hesitation took hold of him. Finally deciding what to do, he ran up the stairs and answered the phone.

"Hello, Mr. Hodges. I'm so sorry to disturb you and hope I'm not interrupting any important task you may be engaged in." Momentarily, he forgot about Cadence as he strained to recognize the voice on the other end of the line. "This is Celia Orth calling." She continued talking as he recognized her as one of the book club members. "Anyway, we were wondering if you would be interested in meeting myself and two others at Harry's Hash House for lunch today." Silence. "Mr. Hodges? Are you still there?"

"I'm sorry, Mrs. Orn was it?"

"Celia Orth."

"I'm sorry, Mrs. Orth. I tell you, this morning has been an extremely busy time for me. I was a little distracted as you were speaking and didn't catch everything that you said. I did manage to get the part about meeting for lunch today, but to my great regret, I will not be able to dine with you and your friends. I have an urgent appointment out of town, and, oh dear Lord, I'm going to be late as it is. Call me tomorrow and we can set up a date for another day." Before Celia could respond, Hodges told her goodbye and hung up the phone, leaving her slightly annoyed.

Celia, who had put the speaker on as she talked, gave everyone a look as if to say, what now fellas?

Damien jumped in quickly. "This may work out even better."

"I don't think so. We don't know how long he's going to be gone, where he's going, who he's seeing, anything," Beth said. "In addition, we won't have anyone with him to warn us when he's coming home."

"Well, scratch that plan. It sounded so good, too," said Jenny.

"We've got to get into that place and find out what's under the basement."

Damien sighed and said, "Looks like we wait until tomorrow and give it another try with Celia. At least he didn't turn her down. That's a good sign."

"I'm sure the old ham is just as eager to be the object of attention as any actor would be, especially the undivided attention from three lovely ladies like us," said Mary, drawing a few sarcastic looks from the others.

Hodges returned to the basement, retrieved the remote and pushed the button for the hydraulic door. It was nearly noiseless as it opened fully and he descended the steps. Choosing an outfit along with accessories, he dressed and retreated from the room, closing the door before he left the basement. As he left the house through the attached door to the garage, he cradled the nightstick in his hands and paused a moment before getting into his car. Quietly and through clenched teeth, he said, "You shall be avenged, my dear Cadence. I promise you."

He started the engine to the car, hit the remote controlling the garage door and was soon on his way to pay Richard Pieson a visit, for he was sure that Richard had killed Cadence, and would now have to suffer the consequences.

"Do you think we should go back into Rochester and do a little snooping in the neighborhood where Cadence and Peltier were killed?" Damien asked. Seemingly out of it for the moment, Beth half-heartily agreed.

" You don't think that's a good idea," Damien said.

"Uh, no. I think it's a great idea," Beth said, suddenly perking up. "I'm thinking we split up, with you going into Rochester while I do some computer searches at home. The detectives might have sent out pertinent security videos to the rest of the law enforcement team and they might have forwarded them to us. If they didn't, I could always contact Sheriff Lewis and I'm sure he would send them out to me."

Damien quickly agreed. He hadn't wanted to say it, but he had been thinking they should split up today to cover more ground. He had discovered in the past few months, however, that he was often better off when most of the ideas came from Beth. She reacted significantly better that way and he was a big boy, so he could handle it.

After kissing Beth, Damien dropped her off at their Stewartville home/office, and he drove back to the Rochester neighborhood. Beth waved goodbye to him from the office door in front and quickly entered the house. She walked through the office and straight to the garage where her Focus awaited. Jumping in the front seat like she was late for her own wedding, she punched the garage remote and tore out of the garage. She didn't know how much time she would have, but she was getting in Hodges' basement one way or another. The drive took her thirty-three minutes.

The Focus came to a crunching halt in front of Hodges' house. No one appeared to be around. She walked quickly to the front door, rang the doorbell and knocked. Gratified there was no answer, she removed her tools from her coat pocket and popped the door open in just a few seconds. She entered and removed her boots on the beautiful welcome rug, and glided down the stairs to the basement. She flipped on the basement light and her own LED flashlight that she kept in her car. Shining the light on the floor and looking for any signs of a seam, she found nothing. Like before, she hopped around on the concrete floor and identified the perimeter where a seam should be visible. Shining the light directly on the area she identified; a small hairline fracture became visible. Her eyes widened just a little as she tried wedging her fingernails underneath the almost invisible crack in the floor. She couldn't do it. She surveyed the room, looking for a screwdriver or pry bar small enough to wedge in the fracture.

Seeing nothing, she jumped on the area in frustration. Letting her imagination run, she tried to think of another way a secret door could open, a hidden button, a lever, a crank, anything. She searched the perimeter walls of the basement and again, came up empty. A moment later, Beth looked on the shelf opposite the stairs and noticed a jewelry box placed in the middle. Well, maybe during his dress up periods he used the contents, or maybe, if she moved the box, the door would open. She strode purposefully to the box and stared at it.

It appeared to be an ordinary jewelry box like the one she had inherited from her mother. It was older, but nicely maintained, and she noticed there was no dust on it. Reaching out with both hands, she held it and lifted the lid slowly. Peeking inside, she was disappointed, jewelry, that's all. What did she expect? She closed the lid and moved the box on the shelf an inch to one side, and then an inch to the other side, all the time watching the fractured area in the floor for movement. Nothing happened.

As she ran her fingers along the shelf she picked up no trace of dust, anywhere. She walked over to the hot water heater and the furnace. She ran her fingers along every surface of exposed appliance, shelf, or sill. There was no dust at all! This guy was seriously ill. He dusted his basement? Who the hell dusts a basement? Well, apparently Gerald Hodges did, because there was not a spec of the stuff anywhere.

She let out a sigh of defeat and frustration. Evidently there would be no grand opening of the secret door today. She had better cut her losses while she still could and get out of there before he came back. Something still bothered her about this entire area in the basement, however. She couldn't quite put a finger on it, but... What was she missing? Maybe nothing, she thought. Maybe there was nothing to miss, she told herself. Maybe Hodges was just what he seemed all along; a peculiar old man who enjoyed dressing up in women's clothing, wearing his mother's jewelry and playing like he was a woman for an evening once in a while. Only she hadn't found women's clothing anywhere in the house.

She walked back over to the jewelry box and opened it again, dug around inside of it, and lifted out what looked like a wedding ring, earrings, and a necklace. Looking more closely, she noticed what looked like the head of a screw sticking up in the middle of the box. It wasn't a screw; it was a sculptured handle. She grasped the handle between the fingers of her right hand and lifted, all the while watching the concrete floor. The floor did not open. She plopped the false bottom down. "Well, that was too good to be true," she said to no one.

She stood contemplating what to do next. Might as well see what's under the false bottom. She lifted the sculptured handle and placed the false bottom holding the rest of the jewelry on the shelf and stared at the object inside. Beth lifted the remote and pushed the open button. She nearly jumped when she realized the floor was rising toward the ceiling. "Oh my God!" she said aloud and watched in amazement and joy at having discovered how to get into the hidden room.

"I'm really quite proud of my engineering feat," came the voice of Gerald Hodges from the middle of the stairway. The floor stopped moving to reveal the steps to the area under the basement, as Hodges descended the remaining distance to the basement floor. "You look quite surprised to see me, Miss Reddy. I hope you are not alarmed."

"I, I don't know what to say, Mr. Hodges. Obviously, you've caught me doing something I shouldn't. And here I am in your house, without your permission, snooping in your basement." She had been shocked to hear his voice. He was dressed in women's clothing, wearing a fashionably cut brown wig with a hint of auburn in it. Sparkling diamond earrings hung from his ears and a gold necklace dangled around his neck.

"Oh, I can tell by your look that you are surprised by my appearance."

"Actually, you look quite lovely, Mr. Hodges," she said feebly.

"Oh my dear, flattery will get you everywhere…except in this case." He passed around the opening in the floor and approached her as she backed up against the wall.

"Please, don't be alarmed. I would merely like to escort you to my favorite room in the house. Please…allow me," he said as he extended an elbow for her to hang onto. Before she took hold of his arm, Hodges added, "I should take the remote, otherwise an accident may happen." She gave the control to him and willingly descended the steps to the hidden room.

His right hand extended in a sweeping motion as he said, "You see. I am quite proud of my collection here. I have evening gowns, pant suits, sweaters, short skirts, which I never wear, mind you. My legs are atrocious and not worthy of display, even though I do shave them regularly. Also, I do not care for the skinny jeans that are the choice of so many women these days. That's something I will never get used to. But, you are welcome to peruse the many items of clothing and accessories I have at my disposal. Please," he encouraged. "Explore."

She let go of his elbow and walked tentatively about the room. His collection of women's clothing was staggering, along with the accessories he had mentioned, scarves, hats, belts, purses. Purses! She noticed the purse that Cadence had reported as stolen six months ago.

"This belonged to Cadence. How did you get it?" she asked.

He hemmed and hawed a bit as he was obviously experiencing conflicting thoughts about what to say. Finally, he said, "It was in the front seat of her car. She left it during one of the book club meetings. I saw it, took the keys out, tossed them on the front seat so she would have a way to drive home, and took the purse."

"So you stole it."

"You could say that."

"I just did. Why?"

Hodges walked around the room in circles before replying.

"You wouldn't understand," he said sadly.

"Try me."

"I loved Cadence, and I needed something of hers to hang onto. I knew she may never be attracted to someone like me. Ha," he said with emphasis and turned his back to her. "When I opened her purse I saw notes she had written to herself, practicing what she was going to say to Laura Walters and Galena Mendez to gain their financial support for her golf sponsorship. I waited several months as she spoke with them, in fact, I heard her argue with Laura one afternoon."

"The day you saw her car, hours before the last book club meeting?"

"Yes."

His voice became agitated as he continued relating what he had heard that afternoon. He had pretended to search for garbage in the neighborhood as they argued. They had been so wrapped up in their heated discussion that his nearby presence hadn't mattered. They never paid any attention to him.

"Cadence was so hurt and angry that Laura wouldn't provide any money to support her in her quest to become the best golfer she could be. Laura, great friend that she was," he added sarcastically, "told her no, that her relatives were not going to support Cadence and she wasn't either. She said that none of them regarded it as a good investment. Laura said she was sorry, but that was the way it was going to be, and that was that. Cadence cried and told Laura it would ruin her life if she couldn't train for the Pro Tour and sobbed uncontrollably as she walked back to her car."

"So that must have been why she hardly spoke at the meeting that same evening."

"I would imagine that's true. Would you, given the circumstances?"

"I suppose not."

Hodges continued his story without encouragement from Beth. It seemed that he wanted to talk, tell her everything and have the full weight of it off his shoulders.

"I was in a rage, although I never showed it to anyone. How could Laura, a friend, ignore Cadence in her greatest time of need?"

"Mr. Hodges, no offense, but, really? Her greatest time of need? She wanted money to go play a game of golf, for Christ's sake. How could you blame Laura or anyone else for that?"

His body trembled as he spoke, "Not just a game, Miss Reddy, a dream was there for Cadence to pursue. It was in her grasp with a little help from her most financially capable friends, and they denied her." The last three words thundered and reverberated throughout the hidden subbasement room.

"You said they. So you killed Galena as well?" Beth couldn't believe she yelled out the question with such emotion, but she was wrapped up in the entire scenario.

"Yes," Hodges said almost in a whisper. "I killed Laura Walters and Galena Mendez because they failed the test of true friendship, and…because I loved Cadence. I did it for her."

Beth swallowed the saliva that had been building up in her mouth and stood silent for several moments. She knew this was a dangerous situation and it had to be handled in the right manner or it was going to end very badly.

"Mr. Hodges, let me help you." His head jerked upward and he looked at her.

"How can you help me, my child?"

She walked nearer him.

"I can go to the police with you and help explain everything. We can do it together and I will support you like a true friend." Hodges appeared to melt a little as his head drooped, but he was silent.

"Will you think about it, Mr. Hodges?" He emitted a long sigh and then he spoke.

"I'm afraid I cannot do that. I know what they will do to me. They'll stick me in some crazy hospital like before, and…" His voice trailed off.

"Please, let me help. I know we can get some good people to see you and… and give you the help you deserve." She placed a hand on his shoulder.

"I'm sorry, it won't work. You see, I know the system, and it's not built for people like me and never will be, but you are so kind to talk to me like this. I appreciate what you've said tonight."

"So, what will you do now, because you know that I have to report what I have learned from you tonight?"

"I know, you have to try something, but I can't allow you to leave tonight."

"Mr. Hodges," she said, shaking her head. "You can't stop me, and furthermore, I don't believe you will even try." She began to walk around him and made it to the bottom of the steps leading to the basement before she felt the electric bite of the taser into her back. Beth collapsed onto the floor as Hodges rushed to ease her fall. Immediate and intense pain coupled with the involuntary contraction of all her muscles had occurred. There was a definite and noticeable increase in her heart rate, undoubtedly caused by the surprise and panic she experienced, as well as the fact that all her muscles were in serious, hardcore contraction.

Chapter 16

"I'm sorry Miss Reddy, but I cannot allow you to leave," Hodges said, with a tinge of sadness to his voice as Beth lay in agony on the floor. He half dragged, half carried her to the far corner of the hidden room and gently arranged her on a thick piece of shag carpeting. He had to act quickly because she would only be debilitated for about fifteen minutes. As swiftly as he could, he went upstairs, found a pillow and several blankets. When he returned, he placed her head upon the pillow and pulled the blankets around her. He tried to remember where the handcuffs were, finally locating them in a box with the remnants of his father's possessions. He had no idea why he had hung onto the antiques for all these years, but was glad that first his mother, and then he had after she died.

He cuffed her to a solid drain pipe that was connected to tiling around the perimeter, which was filled with pea rock. He had made sure that his secret room would not flood when heavy rains fell. Not that that would be a problem in the dead of winter.

When he was satisfied that she couldn't escape, he opened a folding chair that had been propped against the wall, sat, and waited to make sure she was going to be all right. He hadn't wanted this to happen and really hadn't thought anyone would ever find out about the hidden room under his basement. Hodges wanted to ask her how she had found it and what made her suspect its existence in the first place.

Ten minutes passed before Beth stopped groaning and gained a measured use of her limbs and faculties. Automatically, she attempted

146

to move, but found herself restrained by the handcuffs attached to the drain pipe. She jerked hard and only succeeded in hurting her wrist, barely moving the sturdy pipe.

Beth let out a giant sigh before she spoke. "Mr. Hodges, that was extremely painful."

"I'm sorry my dear," he replied apologetically. "But you left me no choice in the matter. I know about your feats, that you were able to kill two people with your bare hands in a fair fight. I'm much older than you and couldn't take the chance of you applying a whipping to me, and then fetching the police."

She raised herself up on an elbow and forearm. "Actually, I only killed one person, and it wasn't with my bare hands. It was with a rock. The other one was shot by Sheriff Cooper Lewis as she was about to kill me."

"Either way, with the skills you have, I'm afraid I would have been defeated had I engaged you in any mortal combat."

Rubbing her side slowly, she replied somewhat lethargically, "Yeah, you would have been." And then she added, "So what happens now? You didn't kill me, so what do you have in mind?"

"First, I would like to find out how you found the door to my hidden room. I thought it was expertly designed with no trace of seams at all. It's incomprehensible to me that anyone would even suspect a door, and yet I arrived home and there you were, comfortably sashaying around my basement with the perfectly hidden door open." As he sat with his chin resting on one hand, leaning forward, he asked, "So, how did you do it?"

She explained how she had noticed the difference in sound as she had walked over the door and her resulting jumping, skipping, and walking over it, trying to establish a perimeter. She told him how she had noticed the hairline fracture, but couldn't get anything underneath it to pry it open, and then eventually discovered the remote.

"Fascinating," he said with admiration in his voice.

"I told you why I suspected the area and how I found it, now you tell me what your next step is going to be."

"I can't tell you what I don't know at this time. For now, you're going to stay down here. The door is well insulated so no one will hear if you decide to yell or scream. I'll make sure you have water and food so you won't waste away. Also, I assume someone, probably Mr. George, knows you came here, so my first order of business will be removing any trace of your vehicle and convince him that you found me here and we talked, but you left for parts unknown. So I've just relieved you of your cell phone and car keys. I'm sorry, your things fell out of your purse when you dropped to the floor." He took the keys and the phone out of his pocket. "I turned your phone off, wouldn't like it traced by GPS or anything like that."

"Mr. Hodges, that's not going to work. Other people knew I had a plan to come here and find this room. They know it exists because this wasn't my first time in your basement."

"You were here the evening Mr. George visited me at the municipal, weren't you?"

"Yes, that's when I discovered the anomaly in the basement floor. I knew I would have to come back and find out why it was there and what was below it. I told Damien and our friends before I came here, so just please give it up and I'll make sure you don't get hurt when this whole thing blows up."

Hodges stood and pondered her words. "If this is true, and I think it is, it changes the equation somewhat, but I am still moving your vehicle and stonewalling any questions that come my way. The police will have to get a warrant to find my room, and by then, I shall be gone, yes…gone." Beth continued to throw objections at him as he ascended the steps to the basement, but it was no use. Hodges was not listening. In a strange way that she really didn't understand, she felt sorry for Hodges and truly wished that no harm would befall him. Beth was more certain than ever that events would not end well for Mr. Hodges.

Gerald Hodges knew that he had to work quickly. It was now dark and he left the house, unlocked her car, and drove east on County Road 4 until it joined Highway 56. Turning east on 56, he drove for a mile before heading south on gravel. He turned off the lights and drove slowly. Hodges found what looked like a good, safe spot a quarter mile from the highway and hit the brakes, easing the car into the ditch off the right side of the road. With the vehicle stuck in the snow, he tried rocking it out of the ditch a couple of times, trapping it more.

Wearing his gloves the entire time so no fingerprints would be found, he opened the driver's door and got out, being careful to obliterate his boot tracks by plowing back and forth through the snow. The ice covered, gravel road wouldn't give up any tracks and he hustled back down to Highway 56 and literally ran to his house in Rose Creek, hoping that no vehicles would pass by. They didn't.

He heard no sounds from the basement and now started making plans to leave the area. Cadence was dead and his work had gone for naught. He thought that someday he would have shared what he had done for her, and maybe she would have loved him for it. But, that was all done now. He had no time to think of the lost possibilities or to grieve for her. As in the past, fight or flight was kicking in and he was given to flight. He would get over her. He always did when a loved one exited his life. He was tough that way, sensitive, but hard. He knew he would find a new love, somewhere.

Damien arrived back at the house, expecting to find Beth deeply involved with computer searches. As he drove into the garage, it was obvious that she was gone. He got out of the car and entered the house, hoping to find a note, since she hadn't called him. No note was attached to the kitchen door; the method they both used when a phone call wasn't made. He tried phoning her, but the call went straight to her voicemail.

Just slightly worried, he decided to have a leftover sandwich and then make a few phone calls to ascertain her whereabouts, hoping that she would save him the trouble by simply calling him, or better yet, walking in the side door. When neither event happened, he called Celia Orth, who also expressed surprise she hadn't called or at least left a note.

"That just doesn't sound like her." She emitted a tiny gasp that was clearly audible on Damien's end of the phone. "You don't think she decided to go back to Hodges' house and snoop around on her own, do you?"

"I'd love to say that she'd never do it, but I can't. I'm going to call Sheriff Lewis and tell him I can't get ahold of her at all and also tell him what we suspect." It was dark and he was beginning to worry more after speaking to Celia. The more he thought about it, Beth was too quick to agree with him when he suggested they split up and perform different chores.

Within thirty-seconds of hanging up the phone with Sheriff Lewis, he was in his car and heading for Gerald Hodges' home. He would be there in half an hour, probably less the way he was driving. Traffic was almost nonexistent as he turned off I-90 onto Highway 56. He depressed the gas pedal as the gauge hit seventy. Don't go crazy and jump to conclusions, he told himself. Beth is a strong woman with a ton of self-defense skills. There was absolutely no way an old man like Hodges could get the drop on her unless her big heart got in the way. If she had a flaw, it was that she trusted some people too much and wanted to believe in them so badly that…she may leave herself open. He loved her for it, but he recognized that it could get her killed in this new business venture they had begun together. He stepped a little harder on the gas, pushing the needle past seventy-five.

Hodges had left the hydraulic door open as he packed his supplies and gathered some food on a plate for Beth.

"Please, Mr. Hodges, please come and talk to me." He had ignored her pleading while doing what he must do, but now relented and descended into the basement and then down the steps to the hidden room. He carried a tray with a chicken salad sandwich on a croissant neatly sliced in half, an orange, a tall glass of water, and a cup of tea.

"Mr. Hodges, I know you think you have your mind made up, but please reconsider everything. You've killed two people and more might be killed if you don't give yourself up."

"More have already been killed," he said with a stony face.

"You mean Cadence…I-,"

"I didn't kill Cadence, or her lover, if that's what you meant, and I didn't mean that they were the only additional deaths."

Beth was struck speechless until she uttered, "Who else did you kill, Mr. Hodges?"

"Someone who needed it. I am positive that Richard Pieson killed Cadence and her lover. Now he is dead as well."

"When, how…?"

"While you were snooping around here. I spoke with Celia Orth earlier today and she wanted to take me to lunch, a rather transparent attempt to remove me from my home so that someone, I figured probably you, could search my house. But I didn't care. I needed to dispatch Mr Pieson. I really didn't think you would find my room, Miss Reddy, so I allotted a certain amount of time for you to search, unsuccessfully I had assumed, and I would hurry back here to find you and Mr. George gone.

"And then I would take my leave in a slightly more relaxed manner than I am now. Please do not think of this as a death sentence, alone in my sub-basement like this. I will leave proper clues for the authorities and Mr. George as to where you are and how to get here, Miss Reddy. I have no interest in killing you." Hodges looked at her admiringly. "You have been a bright, shining star in my life for the past year. I have watched and listened to you at your book club meetings, always with a bit of regret that I was not a younger man who could vie for your hand. I have also enjoyed reading in the newspaper about your past exploits. That is why I was able to prepare the Taser for you, because I knew there would be no way I could ever defeat you in hand-to-hand combat. Not that I would ever try."

Trying to buy more time, Beth asked him another question.

"But Mr. Hodges, why did you kill Richard Pieson? If anything, he was a victim in this whole episode with Cadence, because she had had several affairs. He was the wronged one in their relationship."

"Not everything is as it seems, Miss Reddy. If there were more time, I could tell stories about those two that would astound you. But to make a long story short, Richard Pieson killed Cadence. Of that I am sure, and for that, he had to suffer." He turned and began to leave.

"So you were the executioner of anyone you thought had treated Cadence poorly," she said without raising her voice in anger.

He turned around one last time and simply said, "Yes."

Beth blurted out the next question, "Did you kill your wives in England?"

Hodges stopped dead cold, his back facing her. She noticed a small tremble in his body as he stood ramrod straight, and suddenly feared she had gone too far.

Slowly, Hodges turned to face her. His head was now drooped. It wasn't anger that she saw in his face, but sadness, regret? She couldn't tell, but Beth sensed he was going to reveal much more about his past life.

He walked nearer to her and sat in the chair he had used earlier.

Somewhat tiredly, he began. "My first wife's name was Betty. I purposefully charmed her to marry me because she was rich and, at that time in my life, that was all I was interested in. When we married, I thought she was the most beautiful woman on earth, but I didn't actually think I would ever fall in love with her. However, I did, and for several years we were the happiest people in the world. She put up with me and I put up with her, although there really was nothing I had to put up with as far as she was concerned. Betty was perfect...until she got sick." He sniffled, and there was a pause of several seconds before he spoke again. "Have you ever heard of Endometrial cancer?" He didn't allow her to answer. "It develops in the interlining of the uterus. Adenocarcinoma accounts for 75 percent of the cases pertaining to this type of cancer. There is abnormal bleeding that varies from insignificant staining to hemorrhage. She developed extreme pain in her pelvis and the backs of her legs. At first, the doctors were hopeful, but within months all hope was erased. The doctors told us we had to face the fact that she was going to die. There were pain killers... and me, to help deal with her illness."

He paused again and Beth said nothing. "This went on for such a long time, constant pain... crying. There was nothing to do." He whispered the last words. "One evening I fell asleep in our bed next to her. I had been up all day and most of the night before because she was having difficulty getting into a comfortable position and, like most days, she had cried. I had cried... All of a sudden she just woke up, as lucid as she had ever been and asked me to just...help her let go. I said no, I cannot do that." He was crying now. "She pleaded with me, said

I had to help her. She had asked me this several times before and I always had said I couldn't do it. This time, I was tired, so tired, and in a weak moment, I finally said yes. She lay back and said to do it now, so I… I took the pillow and held it over her mouth and nose until… I don't know…a long time. She didn't even struggle." He sniffed his runny nose as tears dribbled from his eyes. "She went quietly and with all my love."

Beth said no more. She couldn't ask about his second wife, but laid back on the pillow he had arranged for her. He left the light on in the hidden room, but closed the hydraulic door. Hodges wrote a note with every letter neatly spaced and slanted. After all, he had won a penmanship award in the third grade when he had learned cursive writing and was extremely proud of it. He took the note and the remote for the hydraulic door and placed them in the center of his dining room table, illuminated by the light directly above.

He picked up both of his bags and began to leave, but turned back once more and looked at the note and remote control. He put the bags down on the tiled floor, walked to the note and arranged it and the remote a quarter of an inch to the side. His head cocked slightly when he did it, still not satisfied it was perfect. He moved it back again.

"There, I guess it was perfect the first time," he said. He picked up his bags again, walked out the door, making sure to lock it, climbed into his 2008 Buick and drove north.

Damien passed only one vehicle driving away from Rose Creek. He slowed down as he approached the big bend that curved east and seemed to direct traffic into the municipal bar on the left. He gave the parking lot a good look as he passed it, looking for Beth's Focus, and then continued on to where he thought Beth might be; the home of Gerald Hodges.

Nothing much seemed to be happening in the little town as he drove in front of Hodges' house. Beth's car was nowhere to be seen and neither was Hodges. The house was dark except for one light in the kitchen area. To stay warm, he left the engine running as he sat and thought about what he should do next. He found himself thinking of what Beth would do in his situation. She'd probably break into Hodges' house and rip it apart looking for him.

He called Cooper Lewis' cell phone and found out he was on his way with important news. One of the locals had found a car matching the description of Beth's car about a mile and a half out of town, but Beth was nowhere to be found. Lewis was headed there now. Damien put the car in gear and followed Sheriff Lewis' directions. He took a right onto the first gravel road he came upon, thinking it to be the one where Beth's car had been found. Beyond the head of the gravel road he saw other lights and drove toward them.

As his headlamps shown upon the vehicle in the ditch, they illuminated the Ford Focus. His heart sank a little when he realized it was Beth's car. Where was she now?

He pulled his vehicle beyond where the Focus was stuck in the ditch and parked fifty yards farther down the ice-covered road. When he got out and shut the door, the patrolman shouted for him to stay back. He identified himself and was immediately allowed to come forward.

The patrolman had come upon the Focus only ten minutes earlier and had been waiting for word from the higher-ups about what to do. While they talked, another car pulled onto the gravel road and stopped in front of them. Sheriff Lewis stepped out of his car and hurriedly walked toward them, stepping gingerly on the ice as he covered the forty feet separating them.

"Patrolman Stitz, it's Sheriff Lewis from Spirit Grove. I just spoke to Derrick Hansen and he'll be here within five minutes, so you can get back to town."

Stitz, who had known Cooper for fifteen years, thanked him, said good luck, and jumped in his patrol car, leaving Sheriff Lewis and Damien alone until Derrick Hansen showed up.

"Sheriff, this just isn't right. What in the hell would Beth be doing out here on this icy, gravel road?"

"Maybe chasing down a lead when all of a sudden she slides off the road and has to hoof it back into town," Lewis said without conviction.

"Yeah, right. I can see you feel the same way I do. Didn't happen that way. I had told you over the phone that she-we-had an idea of searching Hodges' house for clues. Beth had found something in the basement that just wasn't right and-"

"And you were going to tell the rest of the team when?" Lewis asked, clearly perturbed. His imposing figure seemed to make Damien shrink a little more as he stood beside the hulking sheriff.

Recovering swiftly, Damien added, "We were making plans to inform the rest of you today, after Beth did some more research. She wasn't supposed to go anywhere or do anything without me."

"Maybe she found something in the course of her research that brought her out to this area."

"Maybe, but I'm thinking we should go back to Gerald Hodges' place right now and see what he knows," Damien said, sounding desperate.

"Looks like Hansen is here, so we'll check with him before we go anywhere. He might have some more information for us." Looking at the trail leading from the ditched car to the road, Lewis continued, "It's pretty obvious Beth climbed out of the car and went back and forth a little. Her tracks are messed up, so she must have forgotten something in the car and gone back for it."

Hansen rubbed his gloved hands together to keep them warm as he approached the two of them standing on the side of the road. "Cooper, I've checked with folks in the municipal, as well as people we've interviewed since this started, and no one has had any contact with Beth Reddy today. We've tried without success to contact Gerald Hodges."

"We were thinking we'd better pay Hodges a visit," Lewis said.

"Apparently, he's not home, so good luck with that," Hansen said.

"We were actually thinking of going inside and having a look around his place," Lewis admitted.

"Cooper, without a warrant, anything you find won't be admissible."

"You got Judge Nelson's phone number?" Lewis asked.

Hansen smiled. "Hell! His number? He lives on the other side of town. You head to Hodges' place and I'll get that warrant. Do whatever you've gotta do. We'll find Beth."

"Do you wanna ride with me or drive yourself?" Lewis asked Damien.

"Beth and I've already got one car stuck out here. We don't need to leave another. I'll turn my rig around and meet you at Hodges' house." All three left the gravel road and headed back to Rose Creek, Hansen to obtain a warrant and the other two to break into Hodges' place, if they had to.

Damien pulled beside Hodges' house first and waited for Lewis, who was only a minute behind. He got out when he saw Lewis open the cruiser door.

"Lights are on in the kitchen, Sheriff, but I haven't seen any movement." Lewis looked momentarily at the window.

"Let's get this show on the road," was all Lewis said. Damien followed him as he sauntered up the sidewalk to the front door. He knocked, and when there was no response, Lewis tried to turn the door handle. "Locked," he said. And then he raised his right boot as high as he could get it and gave the door a strong kick. It exploded open.

"I think Beth used a pick to get in," Damien confessed.

"She has her method and I have mine. And by the way I didn't hear what you just said about the pick, got that?"

"Yeah, I got it."

They walked in warily, Lewis with his gun drawn and Damien behind him. Both saw the note and remote control lying on the table. Crossing the ten-foot space between the door and the table, Lewis looked at it without touching anything. He nudged the remote over to read the entire note with a gloved hand, and let out a relieved breath of air.

"It's from Hodges and it says Beth is under the basement." Damien shot a worried look at Cooper.

"Is she alive?"

"The note doesn't say. Just says she's under the basement and to use the remote."

They stood for several moments, dreading what they might find in the basement. Finally, Lewis tapped Damien's shoulder and said to follow. As they descended the basement stairs, the extreme neatness of the entire area escaped them; they were intent on only one thing: finding Beth alive. When they reached the bottom, Lewis and Damien's eyes swept the area for a door as Lewis anticipated hitting the remote control button. They saw nothing.

Finally, Lewis said, "Well, here goes nothing," and he pushed the top button on the remote control. To their surprise, a humming sound was heard, a crack in the floor appeared, and a door rose toward the ceiling.

"I'm here! I'm here!" they heard Beth yell.

Damien rushed down the steps first, with the sheriff following closely.

"He left me cuffed to the drain pipe and then left," Beth yelled. Lewis looked around for a hacksaw.

"I'll check around upstairs and in the garage and be right back," Lewis called as he moved up the steps.

"Beth!" Damien cried joyfully at the sound of her voice. And then his tone changed. "You came here alone. Can you imagine how worried I was when you weren't home when I got there? No note! No phone calls! You can't ever do anything like that again."

"I'm sorry, Damien, but I just had to act right away. The time was right and I couldn't wait. I should have called."

"You should have called and waited for me," he said vehemently.

She looked away, ashamed. "You're right. It was exactly the wrong thing to do and I've learned the hard way." She looked at him again. "It will never happen again. I promise you." He knew she meant it.

Sheriff Lewis came charging down the stairs carrying a hack saw.

"Found it in the garage. Back up, and I'll get her out of those." Damien backed away and Lewis went to work on the cuffs. They were off within a minute.

"Do you have any idea where he went?" Lewis asked Beth.

"I don't know, but it didn't sound like he was ever coming back." She paused for a moment. "Sheriff, he killed Laura and Galena. He said he also killed Richard Pieson."

"Richard Pieson? Not Cadence, or the guy she was with?" Lewis asked.

"No, he didn't kill Cadence or Claude Peltier. He said he loved Cadence and he killed Laura and Galena because they wouldn't help her. Then he killed Richard Pieson because he said Richard had killed Cadence and Peltier."

"It doesn't make sense to me," Damien said. "Did he tell you that?"

"Yes, he did," Beth said, with some exasperation. She related everything he had told her as Sheriff Lewis and Damien listened intently.

"The guy's certifiably crazy," Damien said, shaking his head. Beth rubbed her wrist where the cuffs had bitten into her skin while struggling to wriggle out of them.

"He needs help," Beth said, as she looked at the two of them.

"Help? He needs a mental hospital and then a long jail sentence. It's times like these when I wish Minnesota had the death penalty." Damien spat out the words.

Sheriff Lewis went upstairs to call Derrick Hansen, Rue Shanahan and the Rochester Chief of Police, leaving Damien alone with Beth. Damien's right palm slammed into the wall, "Damn it, we can't let Hodges get away with killing three people, by his count, and doing this to you."

"He could have killed me, Damien, but he didn't."

"Yeah. Why? What went on in his weird, crazy brain?"

"He said I didn't deserve to die so he was leaving me here with instructions on how to find me. He knew the authorities would come to his house looking for me. He could have left me here to die and maybe no one would ever have discovered this place."

"I would have. I would have torn this entire house apart to find you," Damien said angrily.

"I know you would have, but the point is, he could have killed me, but didn't. He has some humanity in there, and he doesn't deserve to die. He did terrible things, but he also suffered through terrible times. I can't argue with his self-admitted confessions, nor would I want to. Laura and Galena were my friends and I'm going to miss them every day for the rest of my life, but Gerald Hodges is not a monster. He's a sick human being who, in his mind, was doing good. He wasn't, but he thought he was. He's mentally ill and needs help." Her look pleaded for him to understand.

Cooper Lewis came down the steps and related the information from Shanahan that a five state alert had been issued for Gerald Hodges, complete with vehicle make, model, and year. A physical description of Hodges had been issued, along with the information that he might try to disguise himself as a woman. The conventional wisdom was that he would be in custody before the following nightfall. In the meantime, he suggested that the two of them go home and get some rest; it had been a stressful afternoon and evening for both of them. He added that deputy Lisa Dolcheski would be joining them so they could cordon off the home off to protect the integrity of the crime scene before the lab specialists arrived.

The flashing red lights of the police and sheriff's vehicles had attracted a small crowd of locals, who were obviously interested in what had happened and literally begging for information. Neither Sheriff Lewis nor Chief Hansen were making any statements to the press, other than that there had a been a break in the murder case and they were pursuing leads on the whereabouts of Gerald Hodges, whom they named as their main suspect in the murders. Nothing was mentioned about Richard Pieson until they could confirm what Hodges had told Beth.

"We'll dust your Focus for prints and then pull it out of here," Derrick Hansen said to Damien and Beth as they started to walk away.

"I know you have to, but I know that Gerald Hodges drove it here to buy himself some time," Beth said. "Although, you probably won't find any prints anyway."

"Yeah, probably not," Hansen agreed. "Too cold out here to go gloveless," he added.

After Damien and Beth opened car doors and settled themselves into Damien's truck, Beth said, "I wonder how long it will be before I get my Focus back."

"I kind of hope it'll be a while. Maybe then you won't be able to sneak off without me." She gave him yet another apologetic look, but didn't say anything; neither one was inclined to speak very much as they headed home to Stewartville.

Chapter 17

"So, if Gerald Hodges didn't kill Cadence Pieson and Claude Peltier, then who the hell did?" asked Derrick Hansen.

"According to Beth, Hodges thought Richard Pieson did."

"I think that's probably bullshit," Hansen said, as he walked up behind Sheriff Lewis. "Most likely, he was just trying to confuse the issue and deflect interest from himself."

"Maybe, but we've got a patrolman checking on Pieson, and he should be contacting me pretty soon," Shanahan said. As if on cue, his cell rang and he picked up immediately. Lewis and Hansen waited, trying to overhear the conversation. After thirty-seconds of noncommittal verbalizations, Shanahan hung up and said wryly, "Richard Pieson's dead. His head was smashed in like the others. Looks like Gerald Hodges wasn't lying after all."

Lisa Dolcheski was applying the yellow crime scene tape around the house while Shanahan, Hansen, and Lewis talked. It was cold and she paused now and then to blow hot air on her bare fingers; she always hated trying to lay the tape out in the cold while wearing gloves. She lacked the dexterity to unroll and tie it up while wearing the city issued gloves, which were stiffer than hell and full of cheap insulation.

"Lisa," Sheriff Lewis called, "give that job to Reynolds. I'd like you to be closely involved in our discussions. It seems like we might have two killers and we need your input."

"Sure thing, Cooper," she said, as she handed the tape to Bob Reynolds, a new beat cop who looked thrilled to be doing anything having to do with a murder investigation.

"Lisa did some ground work for us concerning Scott Walters and his adult children. Please fill these gentlemen in," Lewis commanded.

She related her trip to the Twin Cities and how it seemed neither Mr. Walters nor his children couldn't possibly be involved in the murder of Laura Walters.

"So, from what you know about Scott, is there any possibility he was involved in the death of Cadence Pieson, and if so, what would his motive have been?"

Lisa was leaning against the front porch rail when she answered Hansen's question. "From what I learned about Scott Walters, I would say there is zero chance he had anything to do with Cadence's murder. My opinion is that Gerald Hodges killed her and Claude Peltier. And," she added, "Richard Pieson. When we find Hodges, we find the man solely responsible for all the murders."

"You said it was Hodges that was responsible. What if Hodges was telling the truth about killing Richard Pieson, that Pieson actually killed his wife in a jealous rage?"

Agreeing with Derrick Hansen, Lisa said, "I think he only said that to deflect our attention away from him."

Sheriff Lewis, who had been merely an interested observer in the discussion until now, jumped in, "I'd like to develop a time line so we can determine if Hodges had time to commit the Pieson/Peltier murders. When we re-interviewed Mrs. Stoutmeir the night of Cadence's murder, she provided some information about Hodges' whereabouts that evening that seemed to make it damn near impossible for him to have driven over to Rochester, killed Cadence and Peltier, driven back, and still be spotted making his junk rounds the same night." Lisa didn't say anything, but she shifted her position against the rail.

"Well, that would seem to lend credence to Hodges' story. Even if Richard Pieson didn't kill his wife and Claude Peltier, we're still looking for a second killer," Chief Hansen suggested.

Lisa added her two cents to the discussion. "I don't know about the time line or how Hodges managed to get around it, but my money is still on him for all the killings."

Rue Shanahan spoke. "You seem pretty sure about Hodges, Lisa. Why are you so cocksure that he is the one-and-only killer?"

Lisa softened and consciously lost the overly aggressive attitude. "I haven't been in law enforcement as long as the rest of you, so maybe I'm just showing my lack of experience. Of course, it could be someone else...It's just a gut feeling."

"Lots of cops have been embarrassed by how their 'gut feelings' turned out in the end, Lisa," Derrick Hansen said condescendingly. "We need to keep our minds open to all possibilities and not get fixated on any one scenario."

Realizing the old, established guard didn't like being upstaged, Lisa became more deferential, "You're right, of course. We should be open to everything." Self-satisfied smiles appeared on Hansen's and Shanahan's faces. Cooper Lewis didn't change his stoic expression but instead asked if other prints had been found at the Pieson, Peltier murder scene.

"None, other than Pieson's and Peltier's," answered Shanahan.

"How about blood? Skin? You'd think the victims may have gotten a couple of licks in. Maybe there's traces of the killer's skin under Pieson or Peltier's fingernails, something that the lab boys could get a DNA match," Lewis suggested.

"No skin or blood, other than the victims', is what the techs are saying," Shanahan said.

Lisa tried again. "Whoever did it is one of the neatest killers around, which would seem to indict Hodges, given his proclivity to keep things in place." Hansen looked at her cockeyed.

"I'll give this to you, Lisa, you're persistent as all hell, and you make good points. From what we observed in his house, he's certainly a neat freak. Of course, any killer would try to avoid leaving fingerprints or samples of their blood or skin for us to analyze. Just looking at the bloody scene and the way Pieson and Peltier were arranged on the bed, I'd have to consider Richard Pieson as the murderer, like Hodges said. He could have killed them in a jealous rage and arranged them to make a point. That makes sense to me. Too bad Pieson is dead and can't talk, which makes it all the more important we find Gerald Hodges."

"Gentlemen, I suggest we do a top to bottom search of Richard Pieson's home and look for anything that might tie him to his wife's murder. We can also check cell phone records and see if there's anything there that might help us." When Shanahan finished, he looked at the others and waited for everyone to give their assent. They all nodded.

"I'll check in with the Minnesota State Patrol and find out if there's any progress locating Hodges," Lewis said. All agreed and began to disperse.

Lewis accompanied Lisa Dolcheski to her vehicle. They stopped in front of her driver's side door and Sheriff Lewis spoke in a low tone. "You've gotta watch it around these guys a little bit, Lisa. You don't want to make them look like uneducated cops who have never done this before. They're good professionals with more experience than you. And they have their own instincts, which, I might add, they tend to keep to themselves until they can latch onto something solid." He paused, waiting for Lisa to respond.

"I know Cooper, I caught myself and dialed it back."

"Just to let you know, I tend to agree with you on Gerald Hodges, but the time factor bothers me. If he did the Pieson/Peltier murders, we have to figure out how he did it and still was seen back here around the same time." He drew his breath in and let it out in a slow cloud of steam.

"We'll figure it out, Cooper. It's just a matter of time." The others had driven away as they had stood talking. They separated, Cooper to Spirit Grove and Lisa to Richard Pieson's house.

Damien drove into the garage where they both hopped out of the truck and walked into the house, looking grim and defeated. They hadn't talked for most of the thirty-five minute drive home. As she crossed the threshold of the door, Beth turned to Damien and spoke.

"I'm so sorry for what I put you through. I just didn't think it through." She looked up at him with misty eyes. "Please let it go now.

It will never happen again." He waited a moment before he drew her to him with the big, comforting bear hug she had gotten so used to in the last year, and kissed her briefly but tenderly on the lips. They stood together like that for a long time, rocking from side to side, until Damien took her hand and walked her into the bedroom.

Chapter 18

The wind had risen during the evening and had blown slippery wisps of snow across Highway 56 as he traveled north of Brownsdale. Out of necessity, he had to travel more slowly than he had wanted; he couldn't take the chance of sliding off the highway, getting stuck in a ditch and having to call for help. Hodges had never liked driving in the evening, but having to deal with the dark and slippery roads made it even worse than usual.

He began thinking about Richard Pieson and how he might have been wrong about him. He had confronted Pieson directly before wielding the nightstick and smashing in his skull. Pieson had sworn he hadn't killed Cadence or her lover, Peltier, claiming he had known about the affair for a long time. In fact, he approved. He had desperately insisted to Hodges that they had an open marriage and both were free to indulge themselves with others at any convenient time.

Hodges, poised with his nightstick held above Pieson's head, had listened, progressively getting angrier until, out of sheer disgust, he repeatedly slammed the nightstick into Pieson until he was breathless. With the life oozing out of Richard Pieson, Hodges had stood above him, happy with what he had done.

Now, boxed in by the dark of night and the wisps of snow blowing across the highway, Hodges began having his doubts. What if he were wrong? He began to think that maybe Pieson hadn't killed Cadence, and if so, who had? He could understand how the police would naturally suspect him for the killing of Cadence and Peltier, but, who else may have wanted her dead besides Richard Pieson? There was one person he thought he could trust to help him find the truth. When he reached County Road 30, he turned east and headed for Stewartville. Hopefully, she was there, and more importantly, would help him find Cadence's killer.

Beth and Damien were sound asleep until Beth felt a gentle nudge on her shoulder. She was turned away from Damien and thought he was signaling he wanted to snuggle. A smile crossed her face as she tried to turn to him, but disappeared as she was stopped by a cold hand upon her shoulder. Confused, she opened her eyes to find herself staring at a strange figure kneeling next to the bed. Reacting remarkably fast, her entire body tensed as she propelled herself backward, bumping and waking Damien.

"What…what the hell-what's going on?" Damien said groggily as he tried to sit up, but was restrained by Beth's body leaning against him. A flashlight shined into their eyes, temporarily blinding them from seeing Hodges. They heard tight, quick footsteps moving across the room, and then the overhead light clicked on, making them blink wildly as they tried to focus their eyes and identify the intruder.

"I am sorry to disturb you, but please, I'm here because I trust you and need your help," Hodges said as he pointed the 45 caliber Smith & Wesson revolver toward them.

Damien yelled, "Help you! What the hell? You kill three people that we know about, probably two more, taser Beth and hold her prisoner, break into our home, hold a gun to our heads, and say you want our help?" Hodges maintained his composure and spoke softly.

"I admit I killed three people," and then he added emphatically, "but I didn't kill Cadence or Claude Peltier. After thinking about it, I don't think Richard Pieson killed them either, and I feel a twinge of guilt having murdered him."

"A twinge? That's cool of you, a twinge," Damien said after having calmed down a bit. Beth, who was still leaning against Damien's body with her mussed hair falling across her face, looked at Hodges.

She said calmly, "Mr. Hodges, put the gun down and we can talk."

"I'm sorry, not just yet. I need to know what you know about Cadence and Peltier's deaths."

"Or what, you'll shoot us, or better yet, bash our skulls in with your nightstick?" Damien said. "And if we do tell you anything, you'll kill us anyway."

"Please... Gerald, put the gun down, and I promise we'll talk."

"You called me Gerald. That's what Lucille called me. It was always Gerald, 'Dear Gerald.' That woman was such a beautiful person to put up with me and all my quirks. And believe it or not, I have many of them." Damien rolled his eyes when he heard that one.

"All right, I'll lay the gun on the night stand as we talk. You two stay in bed and we may yet accomplish something. Deal?" he asked.

"Deal," Beth said emphatically. Damien, screaming internally, said nothing, but nodded his head.

"Splendid," Hodges said as he placed the gun on the table next to where he sat. Damien noticed it was still within Hodges' reach.

Beth told everything they knew about the murder of Cadence Pieson and Claude Peltier as Hodges listened, never taking his eyes off her face. When she was finished, she asked Damien if she had forgotten anything. He shook his head no.

They sat with no one speaking for what seemed an excruciatingly long time, but in reality the silence had lasted only momentarily.

Leaning forward, Hodges postulated, "It would appear that the person who killed Cadence and Peltier used a similar method to mine. I suggest to you that someone is trying to pin their murders on me to cover up their own crime. We simply have to figure out who that person is."

"Yeah, that's all, just figure it out," Damien laughed.

Beth spoke. "Whether they knew they were pinning it on you personally or not is up for debate, but I agree they may have taken advantage of what you did in Rose Creek and Austin thinking their murders would be connected. You were known in law enforcement circles as a 'person of interest,' but not to the general public, except for a few of your old friends in Rose Creek."

"Don't forget Mrs. Stoutmeir, who seemed to suspect Gerald here from the get go," Damien countered. He had used Hodges' first name sarcastically.

"That's a little unfair, Damien, to say she suspected Gerald of Laura's murder. She only said that he may know something because of his travels around town." Beth kept using his full, first name to constantly remind Hodges of her interest in him.

Clearly buoyed by how the conversation was going, Hodges asked Beth a question.

"Do you think any other members of your book club could possibly have killed Cadence and Peltier?"

She turned her head a millimeter sideways, assuming a contemplative look. After a few moments, Beth said, "I have a real hard time believing any of the ladies in the book club would commit murder. I don't think so," she said, a little unsure of herself.

"Please keep an open mind about that," Hodges implored. "It may be someone involved in the book club who held a grudge against Cadence, maybe jealous of her, or, or, or…"

"Hodges, you watch way too much TV. You've got an overactive imagination and you're grasping at straws," Damien said, as he leaned back and crossed his arms. Hodges smiled knowingly.

"What's the smile about, Gerald?" Again, Damien said the name in a sarcastic tone

"Junior," Hodges began condescendingly, "There is much you do not know when it comes to life. Perhaps you will allow me to be your teacher, mentor, if you prefer, about the seamier side of life."

"I can see what you mean. You appear to be an expert regarding the seamier side."

"Damien!" Beth said curtly. "Just cool down. This is getting us nowhere. Gerald, do you suppose Damien and I could get dressed and we could move to our living room to discuss this? I feel just a little uncomfortable talking about this while I sit in bed, half naked." Hodges agreed quickly.

"Forgive me. I got wound up in our conversation and didn't give it a second thought. Of course you may change. Go right ahead." Damien and Beth looked at each other.

"Uh, could we have a little privacy while we throw some clothes on?" Damien asked Hodges.

"I do not think it would be wise of me to take my eyes off either one of you. I sense that our relationship is still a bit tenuous and not as forthright as I know it will become. In deference to Ms. Reddy, however, I will avert my eyes as best I can, but you shall have no such luck Mr. George." They were as discreet as possible as they threw on the clothes they had worn last night, and then all three moved into the living room. Hodges had picked up his revolver and followed them at an appropriate distance. Crazy thoughts of getting the drop on Hodges passed momentarily through Damien's brain but evaporated when he considered that Beth might get shot in the process.

After they were comfortably ensconced on the sofa and two chairs, Hodges laid down the pistol, this time a little further out of his reach. Whether he was signaling Damien and Beth his trust in them was deepening or it was just an oversight was a matter of debate.

Beth looked at Hodges while she said, "Gerald, you and I talked quite frankly when we were in the hidden room under your basement. You told me everything, including that you loved Cadence, and that you committed the two murders because Laura and Galena wouldn't help her. Your love for Cadence is what drove you to kill and you thought you were doing Cadence a great service." Hodges bowed his head low as she talked. "Damien does not have the same level of knowledge or trust in you that I have; that is obvious. If we're going to help you find whoever murdered Cadence and Claude Peltier, you're going to have to tell us everything, and you're going to have to give the gun to Damien."

Damien's head turned quickly toward Beth. Hodges considered what she had said only a moment before he picked up the gun, walked it over to Damien and handed it to him, butt end first. Damien, slightly unsure of this development, accepted the gun and held it gingerly.

"Please don't drop it. Might go off, you know," Hodges said seriously. And then he added, "I have to confess, it's not even a real gun." Damien checked the remarkably clever copy of a 45 revolver and nodded to Beth that Hodges was telling the truth. He laid the plastic revolver on the coffee table between them.

"Mr. Hodges," Damien began, "how did you know where we lived?"

"I googled Beth's address a while back. I then used my GPS to get here tonight."

"And your car? Is it parked out front?"

"No, I took the liberty of parking it in your garage."

"But how did you get in? There's a security code you have to input," Beth asked.

Hodges sighed a little as he said, "You are not the only one with breaking and entering skills, Beth." Damien had to admit he was right about that.

"One more thing, Gerald, if we are going to help you find the person who murdered Cadence, then you have to promise you will turn yourself in to the police." Hodges looked unsure of himself.

Finally, he said, "If we find the person responsible, I will."

"Are you okay with this, Damien?" Beth asked. He looked at Hodges, back to Beth, and then let out a huge sigh. "I can't believe I'm saying this, but all right. I'll trust both of you, for now."

Chapter 19

Lisa arrived at Richard and Cadence Pieson's well appointed home near the local community college just in time to observe Richard's body being removed from the premises. She said a quick hello to Rob Whittman, one of the technicians, and went inside to search for anything that might help her on the case.

Pieson's body had been outlined in chalk next to a bloodstained sofa. Lamps and tables had been tipped, and broken glass was scattered throughout the living room where the body had been found. Must have been quite the struggle, she thought.

A few moments later she found herself ignoring the carnage in the room and looking through file cabinets, notebooks, nightstands- anything that could shed some light on a connection between Richard Pieson and the murders of Cadence and Peltier. She stayed for an hour looking for evidence indicating Richard could be involved. She found nothing.

She decided to call it a night, passed through the living room where Rob Whitman was now working, and said goodnight. He waved half- heartedly and continued on with his laborious job.

It seemed like it had warmed up since she arrived, and indeed, a warm front had moved in during the late evening, as the local weatherman had predicted. She stood on the front porch area of the Pieson home and drank in the scene that encompassed one of the brightest, starry skies she had ever seen in southern Minnesota. Lisa pulled her gloves on and strode to her official vehicle. The starlight reflected off the hood of the car, giving it a waxy sheen that made it look cleaner than it actually was. When she opened the driver's side door, Lisa was reminded that she was not in possession of a 'clean' vehicle, at least not on the inside. Papers and a half-full thermos bottle lay scattered on the floor and front seat of the car. She remembered her mother saying something like she would never attract a man if she stayed as sloppy as she was. No mom, I probably won't. Lisa started the car and drove around the half-circle parking area to begin the drive to Spirit Grove.

She turned left out of the driveway and onto the frontage road leading to I-90. Thoughts of the earlier conversations with Rue Shanahan, Derrick Hansen, and Cooper Lewis ate at her. She hated the fact that she had to defer to the condescending, conventional wisdom of her male superiors. She was especially upset that they hadn't bought into her "gut feelings" and instead, had denigrated her for expressing them. As she turned right onto I-90 and traveled east, Lisa wondered how she could convince the others of the absolute guilt of Gerald Hodges.

Manufactured evidence? To accomplish that would require her to deliver some sort of physical connection tying Hodges to the Pieson/Peltier murders. That was probably too tricky of a task for her to accomplish at this point. No, she would have to continue to rely upon her constant stressing of Hodges' probable guilt. She knew that if you repeated a falsehood often enough it would come to be regarded as fact by most people. She would bend and twist every bit of circumstantial evidence to steer it toward Gerald Hodges. This was going to be more difficult than she had assumed.

A vision of Claude's face rushed to the front of her mind. Such a poor, stupid, boy he was. After a month or two, she couldn't even enjoy sex with him because he was unimaginative and lacked interest. So, she wasn't the least bit sad when he stopped taking her phone calls and changed his locks, although, that could never keep her out of his apartment. And then there was Cadence. Now that was the proverbial straw that broke the camel's back. To be dropped in favor of Cadence? She could never let that stand...never.

It just so happened that someone had decided to go on a killing spree of book club members, which coincided with her desire to wreak a little revenge on Claude and Cadence. It was a perfect storm of events that allowed her to take her vengeance. All she had to do was copy the MO of the book club murders. She hadn't even been sure until recently that Hodges had been the killer, but in the end, it made little difference. She had just tried to follow the pattern.

Her disgust with Cadence and Peltier caused her to add her own twist; arranging the bodies in a loving embrace. How sweet to see the lovers entwined in death! It had not been hard to pull the bodies onto the bed and prop them up, although she had to use a lamp cord to tie them together so they wouldn't keep sliding apart. That had taken a bit of effort to accomplish, but she was satisfied with the result.

Lisa felt more and more confident she could pull this off. Everyone was now certain Hodges had killed Laura Walters and Galena Mendez. It certainly wasn't a stretch to think she could convince the other law enforcement personnel that he was also guilty of killing Cadence and Peltier. Hodges was a strange patsy who just fell into her lap, allowing her to take care of Peltier and Cadence. It was Karma. Had to be.

There had been no way Cadence was ever going to leave that apartment alive, especially after recognizing Lisa. In a very strange way, she had wanted Cadence to recognize her and realize what was going to happen. Lisa's heart raced faster as she relived the moment when her nightstick went crashing into Cadence's skull. Take that, bitch! You won't ever mess with my man again. "My former man, anyway," she said aloud.

Soon, Lisa realized she was back in Spirit Grove and slowed her car as she approached the stop sign on Main Street. Looking to her right, she noticed the lights were on in Cooper's office. Might as well go in and find out if Hodges had been picked up yet.

She parked her car, walked gracefully to the law enforcement office, and opened the door. Cooper Lewis was sitting at his desk with his reading glasses perched upon his nose. He looked up and greeted Lisa.

"So how'd it go at Richard Pieson's house?" he asked.

"I didn't find anything in the short time I was there that might connect him to Cadence and Peltier's murders, but my money is still on Gerald Hodges." Lisa said.

"I know you're convinced of it, Lisa; but that timeline thing still bothers me. For the life of me, I just don't see how he was able to do it and get back in time for Mrs. Stoutmeir to see him when she says she did.""Maybe Mrs. Stoutmeir is too old to remember exactly when she saw him, Cooper. Some older people tend to get confused you know."

"She doesn't seem like the type to get confused, and has demonstrated that she's observant. Also, she's been right on with everything else she told us. To tell you the truth, Lisa, I don't get why you keep debunking anything that might clear Hodges of Cadence's murder." He looked her squarely in the eye as he sat back in his easy chair. "Do you know something you're not telling me, Lisa?"

"No, of course not," she said huffily. He studied her face intently for several moments and then gathered up the papers he had been reading and handed them to her.

"We got some information this afternoon while we were out. When you read it, you might change your mind about Gerald Hodges." She accepted the stack of papers he handed her and saw they were police and medical reports from England.

"Read them tonight if you get the chance." He plucked his hat and coat off the hanger near the door and began to walk out of the office. "I'm going home to get a good night's rest. Read that with an open mind, Lisa. Hodges might still be our man, but something about Cadence and Peltier's murders just doesn't feel right to me." He gave her a sly look. "Call it a gut feeling." And he walked out.

For the first time in the last several days, Lisa began to experience fear that she would be caught. She knew that look from Cooper, the one where he showed doubt about the veracity and trustworthiness of another person; that look appeared to be focused on her.

Chapter 20

"And so, where do we begin?" Hodges asked as he rested his hands on his knees.

"I suggest we look at all the book club members again," Damien said.

Beth acted as if she was going to tear her hair out. "We've reviewed everyone in the book club at least twice. I just don't see any of them having anything to do with the murders of Cadence and Peltier. I mean, seriously? Carin Loggerton, guilty of being a murderer? Brenda Edinsel, a teacher? Penny Scheid? Are you kidding me?"

"It is my contention that under the right circumstances, anyone is capable of murder," Hodges interjected. He then resumed lining up the knick knacks on the coffee table between them.

"I would agree, Gerald, but come on. I've known these women for a couple of years now. There's no way any of them would kill Cadence or Claude Peltier."

Hodges looked up from his rearranging and said, "Well then, we will have to look elsewhere, won't we?"

"The trouble is we don't have an elsewhere, Gerald," Damien said.

"Please call me Gerry or Mr. Hodges. I like to reserve Gerald for special people such as Ms. Reddy here."

"All right, G e r a l d," Damien strung the name out to show his displeasure. "But we still don't have any other suspects, since you murdered Richard Pieson."

His head hung low as he said, "I admit I probably killed the wrong person in a fit of passion. After I had time to reflect upon the situation and consider Mr. Pieson's abject denial of any involvement in Cadence's murder, I reconsidered his guilt."

"A little late for Mr. Pieson, don't you think?" Damien said with a tinge of cruelty in his voice.

"I will regret my actions concerning Mr. Pieson for the rest of my life."

"Easy to say," Damien said under his breath.

"This is getting us nowhere. I should give Cooper Lewis a call and find out if there are any more leads they've come up with," Beth said. "I'd like to find out if they gleaned anything from the security cameras in Peltier's apartment building."

"Capital idea," Hodges said enthusiastically.

"Better wait a while, Beth. It's three-fifteen in the morning, and I don't think Sheriff Lewis will appreciate a call just yet," Damien said.

Beth reflexively looked at her left wrist where her watch would normally be strapped, but diverted her gaze to the clock hanging on the wall over the flat screen TV. Hodges twisted his body around to view the clock.

"I believe it was you, Beth, who stated that only law enforcement personnel knew the details of the murders I committed."

Beth looked distressed. "That's not entirely a true statement," Beth said. "One of our members gave all of us a pretty detailed report the next day at a meeting in Austin." A frown appeared on her face.

"So, one of your members of the book club could have copied the method I used and utilized it to kill Cadence and Peltier," Hodges suggested. "Do any of the other members hold a grudge against Cadence?" he asked.

"Everybody loved Cadence. This is a dead end," Beth answered.

"Think! One of them must have had something against her," Hodges said desperately.

"No, I'm sure of it. No one in the book club could ever kill her."

"We need to see the security tape of Peltier's apartment," Damien interjected. "It has to show someone entering or leaving the area. Maybe you, Hodges."

Hodges snapped his head toward Damien, looking as if he might charge across the coffee table separating them and attack. Damien flashed a look that told Hodges he would relish the attempt. It must have been enough because Hodges immediately recovered and appeared to relax a little. Damien felt slightly disappointed that Hodges pulled back.

Sensing the tension between Hodges and Damien, Beth said, "You know, I'm hungry. Why don't we go to the kitchen and Damien can fix us three fantastic omelets? His omelets are the greatest." She looked hopefully at the two of them.

Hodges immediately agreed, stating that his hunger knew no bounds. Damien made it clear he didn't appreciate the suggestion, but acquiesced as he held an arm out waving Hodges and Beth into the tight-fitting room. Hodges followed Beth into the kitchen with Damien close behind. Thoughts of overpowering Hodges continued to plague Damien as they entered the kitchen. He had the perfect opportunity now, but he knew if he did, Beth would never forgive him.

She seemed to have established some weird kind of bond with Hodges that he couldn't possibly understand, at least just yet. He worried because they were harboring a confessed murderer. In fact, they were helping him. None of the local law enforcement-hell, no law enforcement personnel-would ever trust them again. It could be construed that they were accessories to a crime. Harboring a fugitive? They could go to jail for what they were doing, and by the way, what the hell were they doing? He had no idea, but whatever it was, it had better turn out right.

Damien busied his mind and body making the delicious concoctions he was famous for in their two-person household: three-egg omelets with diced ham, green and red peppers, onions, pepper jack cheese, and a special sauce that his mother had taught him how to make when he was a child. After artfully folding the ingredients into the first omelet, he expertly folded it over at just the right time, making a near perfect specimen. The sauce was simmering next to the burner where he was making the omelets. He flipped the first omelet on a plate and ladled sauce over it.

Hodges was engaged in lining up the knives and forks on each place setting while Beth retrieved a bottle of orange juice from the refrigerator and poured a generous amount into each glass.

"Go ahead, start," Damien told Hodges in the voice tone of one who was not pleased to be doing what he was doing. Hodges, to Damien's dismay, never noticed the sarcasm in his voice and dug right in.

"Delicious, Junior. Uh, please excuse me, Mr. George. I apologize for lapsing into the moniker that my friend, Earl Mancoat, had given you." Damien sighed, but didn't say anything as Hodges chewed enthusiasticlly, obviously enjoying the eggs. Beth ate her omelet efficiently without saying a word, while Damien finished cooking his, flipped it onto a plate, and then began devouring it as if he hadn't eaten all day.

After they had finished, Hodges suggested that if Beth was absolutely confident that no other member of the book club was involved in Cadence's death, then it could only be someone in the law enforcement area who had been aware of the details of the other murders.

"They would have to be intimately involved in all of the details of the murders in Rose Creek and Austin," Hodges asserted.

"You mean the murders you committed," Damien reminded him.

"Yes, the murders I committed." Damien and Hodges stared at each other for several moments until finally, Hodges turned away and said with an obvious tone of remorse, "I am not proud of what I have done, Mr. George. In some ways I am as much a victim as the people I murdered." Damien scoffed.

"I know Ms. Reddy has as good a reason as anyone to hate me for what I did to her friends." Beth's face was impassive. He took a deep breath, exhaled slowly and then looked directly at her. "I am not a monster but only a man ruled by curious trappings of the mind that I do not understand. I've lived with these…anomalies of the mind, for all my life. At times I've come to grips with what I am, but, still, much of what I do is done out of sheer necessity to ensure my survival in a world I am poorly suited for." He placed his head in his hands as he bowed forward. "This is probably the most I have spoken about myself since my first stint in a hospital, where I gained hardly a scintilla of self-understanding."

"Gerald, how did you happen to be admitted to the hospital?" Beth asked.

He laughed a little before he answered her question.

"My parents placed me there after several incidents at school and home. It was known as a mental hospital then, and frankly, I don't even know if it is in existence anymore." Continuing, he said, "I…didn't seem to get along very well with other children. The hospital staff deemed me intellectually deficient and unable to learn how to socialize properly with others. My parents and I knew that wasn't true. After all, I was able to figure out square roots of numbers when I was five and was reading classic novels by age seven. That didn't seem to convince the good doctors at the hospital, who at one time classified me as an idiot savant. After a year in the hospital, where I was also schooled, I was released back to my parents and they raised me as best they could."

"You mentioned that was the first time you were hospitalized. What about the other times?" Beth asked.

"Time. Only one more time. It seems that I was able to function fairly well when I returned home after that first hospitalization. I attended school, church, and community events. Life was not easy and I certainly had difficulty with other children. It seems like I did not fit in any social group.

College was slightly better. At least there I was able to focus on my studies without being teased by others. College students are a little more mature and tended to classify me as just a little weird, so they steered clear of me. I graduated with a degree in physics, but after graduation I decided to attempt something out of the box, eventually joining the Merchant Marine as a shipboard engineer."

"You didn't have any problems with others who worked on the ships you served on?" Damien asked.

Hodges hesitated before answering. "There were none worth mentioning. I served for twenty years without serious incident and then retired, joined an acting company in England and married a wonderful woman who I met there." Beth gave a knowing nod of her head, remembering Hodge's story of her illness and death.

"You mean, Betty?"

"Yes. After Betty's death, the authorities checked me into a hospital where I received counseling to deal with what had happened."

"Whoa, what do you mean? How did Betty die?" Damien asked.

Beth put a hand on Damien's knee. "I'll explain later."

Hodges continued, "The best thing that came out of it was my second wife. She was in my counseling group, where we bonded and later married. It seems like I was snake-bitten in the ways of love."

"And what do you mean, snake-bitten?" Damien asked.

"She was sick, as well. That's why she was in the counseling group, to help her cope with what would eventually come. I won't bore you with the name of the disease, but, suffice it to say, we had three years together and then she passed away." He was silent for several moments.

Damien began to feel slightly disgusted with himself as a small twinge of sympathy for Hodges crept into his brain. He really didn't want to feel anything other than contempt for this man who had murdered at least three people, but tiny inroads of pity began to wend their way into his thoughts. He hoped he wasn't being played; God he hoped not.

"Gerald, we know about your life with Lucille, but why Boston? Why did you leave England and settle in Boston?" Beth inquired.

He frowned a little and shrugged his shoulders. "Why not Boston? It seemed like a good area for a fresh start. I thought if I returned to America I might establish a life worth living in the country I was born, and it seemed to fit my desire to be just another faceless, nameless citizen.

When I met Lucille, it was as if I had met an even more perfect woman than I had before. I don't know why, but in a way, I've had incredibly good luck in meeting wonderful women. Unfortunately, I've never been able to remain attached to one. Lucille, as you obviously know, didn't have an incurable disease but she had me, which seemed to be just as bad. I tried my best to be "normal" for her, but I will never be normal. That is very obvious to anyone who knows me. Anyway, you know it didn't work out."

"You know she still has feelings for you, don't you, Gerald?"

He smiled, acknowledging he knew what she had said was true.

Chapter 21

The sun had risen at 7:33. It had been a cold night with temperatures dipping below zero for the entire state of Minnesota. Derrick Hansen had awakened before dawn and driven into work far earlier than usual. The evening before he had been informed that the tape on Peltier's apartment building security cameras had been acquired and viewed by the Rochester police. He had also been told a breakthrough may be imminent. Hansen had invited Sheriff Cooper Lewis and Chief of Police Rue Shanahan of Austin to meet him in his Rose Creek offices by 9 a.m., so they could review the tapes together.

Sheriff Lewis had asked that Beth Reddy and Damien George also be present for the tape viewing. Reluctantly, Hansen had acquiesced and called them as soon as he had arrived in his office. He continued to hold Ms. Reddy and Mr. George in low regard but had not made any kind of stink about including them in the investigation. His thought was that anyone could get lucky, like Ms. Reddy had, in the discovery of Hodge's hidden room under the basement. It had been the break they had needed to solve the three local murders, and probably the Cadence Pieson and Claude Peltier murders as well.

Hansen had wanted to view the tapes before the others had arrived, but Cooper Lewis spoiled his plan by showing up at 8:30.

"You're early Coop. What gives?"

"Anticipation. That, and I couldn't sleep worth a damn last night."

"Where's Lisa? I figured she'd wanna be here to nail her favorite suspect and gloat like hell that it confirmed her gut feeling."

"I didn't bother to call her about this. Just left a note saying I'd be over here for a meeting of the chiefs." He cut a brief laugh.

"That's too bad," Hansen said sarcastically as he dropped his own, curt laugh.

"I wish you would treat her better, Derrick. She's a very good officer and I wouldn't want anyone else watching my back. In my mind, she's got it all, brains, brawn, skill, instincts, and, she's a good looking blond."

"Yeah, I have to say, there aren't many of those in law enforcement these days-the good looking blond part, anyway."

"One thing I don't quite understand is why she's so hellbent on the idea that Hodges killed Peltier and Cadence Pieson. We've talked about the timeline thing and she just keeps sticking to that one-track idea of hers that Hodges somehow did it, regardless of accounting for the distance and time problems. She's stuck and can't come up with any other plausible explanation."

"Well, just to let you know, the Rochester police think the security tape from the apartment building may have provided us with a breakthrough and I'm more than ready for that," Hansen said.

"How about you offer me a cup of your kick-ass coffee and we'll try to enjoy it until the others arrive." Lewis said, winking at Hansen. The reference to the kick-ass coffee was an inside joke between the two of them, as they both knew that Hansen made the worst coffee in the world, even worse than Lewis'.

Soon, they were discussing their own pet theories about the Peltier/Pieson murders and drinking a cup of coffee that could generously be labeled awful.

Rue Shanahan entered the office just before nine. Reddy and George pulled in five minutes later. An employee of the apartment building also joined them to help identify the comings and goings of residents on the digital security tape.

After pulling off their heavy coats and complaining about the extreme cold outside, they gathered in the only room that would accommodate the number in their group and began to watch the tape.

Nearly ten minutes passed with no one of interest identified. Before fast forwarding to the time of interest, the apartment complex employee mentioned several known residents who had entered and left at least three hours before the murders had taken place. Finally, Cadence appeared entering the apartment building and also leaving the elevator at Claude Peltier's floor. A gap that they fast-forwarded through on the digital tape revealed no other movements until an hour later. A hooded figure of a woman, or what seemed to be a woman, appeared at the entrance door of the apartment building and punched in several different combinations of numbers to gain entrance.

"I don't recognize that person," said the apartment house employee.

"Back up the tape and freeze it on her," Hansen said.

"Can you magnify the image and get a close up?"

"I can zoom in a little." The hood of the unisex coat still obscured the person's face, but the hands appeared to be long and the fingers too thick to be a woman's.

"Ok, let it go and we'll see where she reappears," Hansen ordered.

They watched the tape as the elevator on the third floor opened, but it wasn't the same figure departing.

"That's Sheila Kupric; she's in 308." The forty year old tenant was dressed in her bathrobe and was clutching a cup of coffee, which she evidently had filled in the lobby on the first floor.

"What happened to our friend in the hooded coat?" Cooper Lewis asked.

"Our friend will resurface pretty soon. There!" The hooded figure appeared at the head of the stairwell on the third floor, walking like a man, the face still obscured from view. "Our cameras cover every floor, elevator, and stairwell. I'll zoom up on the head and you'll see a grainy image, like the person put something over his or her face." He froze the picture and zoomed in on the person's head. Blond hair was visible near the bottom of the hood, sticking out and curling under the chin.

"It's like a woman with a stocking over her face," Damien said. Hansen shot him a look as if to say, "Speak when spoken to." He said no more.

Cooper Lewis, who had been watching the figure intently said, "Release the frame. I wanna see her walk again." The figure definitely walked like a man as it headed directly to Claude Peltier's room and appeared to pull a tool from a pocket, opened the door within seconds and vanished into the room.

"Looks like we have our killer who looks vaguely like a woman, but walks like a man," Hansen stated.

"Sounds a lot like Gerald Hodges to me. The women's clothing found in his sub basement and his previous killings match the MO. I'll bet if we match the height indicated on the tape to Hodges that it'll be the same."

"It's not Hodges," Lewis stated, exhaustion in his voice.

"Still clinging to your timeline theory?" Shanahan asked

"No," Lewis replied angrily. "Back the tape up to when she enters the third floor and watch her walk again."

The apartment employee did as he was told.

"Looks like a man walking to me. I hate to say it, but Lisa should be here right now just so she could say I told you so to each of us. Damn it, I don't like it when someone else's gut instincts are better than mine," Hansen confessed.

"It's not a man?" Beth asked while looking at Cooper, who just stared at the screen with a deflated look in his eyes.

"No. It's Lisa," Cooper said sadly.

"What? Are you kidding me? Lisa Dolcheski, your deputy? What the hell are you saying Cooper? Lisa's our killer? Why?" Hansen had almost sounded hysterical as he spat out each question in staccato fashion.

The room was silent for a minute, waiting for Cooper Lewis to state his case as to why he thought it was Lisa.

"I've seen that walk for the past seven years; it's Lisa. I couldn't stop wondering why she wanted so much to tie Hodges into the Peltier/Pieson murders. Finally, this makes sense. For whatever reason, she killed Cadence and Peltier and tried to conveniently pin them on Hodges."

"Are you sure, Cooper?" Beth asked.

He looked at her and said directly, "Yes."

"We'll pick her up, Cooper. I'm assuming she's minding the store in Spirit Grove," Hansen said.

"She is… But no, don't. I'd like to bring her in myself. She's my deputy and I need to do it. I want to do it," Lewis said emphatically. Shanahan asked if he needed backup and Lewis refused.

"She'll come with me, and there won't be any trouble," Lewis said. With that, he picked up his Stetson, put his coat on, and walked out into the cold while the others stood watching him.

"He seems awfully sure of himself," Hansen commented to the others.

"He's worked with her a long time, and I'll bet he has other observations about Lisa he didn't tell us about," Shanahan replied.

Damien interjected a comment. "He might have suspected her before he even saw the security tape."

"That would help explain his subdued, tired reaction when he saw her in the apartment tape. It's like he just had to confirm his earlier suspicions." Beth said.

"Well, whatever. It looks like we'll have both our murderers in custody and wrap both cases up soon. Which reminds me, we haven't had any word on Hodges. I'm surprised we haven't picked up that looney yet. It won't be long. Now that's what my gut instinct tells me," said Hansen.

Damien and Beth tried to hide the uncomfortable feelings they harbored because they were not at all sure that Hodges would still be in their house when they returned. They wanted to remove themselves from the Rose Creek police station as quickly as possible to make sure he was still at home, but found Hansen and Shanahan suddenly acting strangely, friendly towards them. They must have been in a celebratory mood because they insisted that Damien and Beth take part in a Diet

Coke toast to solving the cases; they did so while itching to get the hell out of there.

Finally, Damien said they had to go and Beth quickly concurred. They hopped in their car and drove as fast as the law would allow back to Stewartville. They were relieved when they saw Hodge's car still in the garage and ran into the house to make sure he was there.

Hodges had been straightening everything in the office and rearranging furniture in the living room. He stopped abruptly when they entered the house, searching their faces for information. He didn't have to wait long.

"We know who killed Cadence." Hodges' face became a stern, chiseled rock as he waited for a name to spill off Beth's lips. When it didn't come fast enough he commanded the answer.

"Who?"

Damien, sensing it might not be exactly the right time to reveal the killer's name, said, "We don't actually know for sure, but Sheriff Lewis thinks he knows the killer and he's gone to arrest her."

"Her?" Hodges asked.

"It's being taken care of Gerald, and now it's time for you to fulfill your part of the bargain."

Hodges hesitated, seemingly unsure of what to do.

"I, I, I, I cannot turn myself in until the killer is in custody. I simply cannot allow it. I've got to see this person and know that she is actually behind bars."

"Look, it's going to happen! Sheriff Lewis has gone back to Spirit Grove to arrest this person and bring her in. You can be assured of it."

"I have been around enough law enforcement personnel to be assured of nothing of the sort. Tell me who it is," Hodges demanded. Beth was about to give him what he wanted when her cell phone rang.

"Ms. Reddy, it's Chief Hansen from Rose Creek. I just received a call from Cooper and it's not good. When he confronted Lisa and tried to persuade her to come back to Austin with him, she went berserk and I don't really know how it happened, but Cooper's been shot." A torrent of emotion flushed through Beth as she listened. "He's going to be fine, but for now, Lisa's on the loose and we're putting out an APB on her. Just wanted to keep you informed." When no words came from Beth he asked, "Are you okay?"

"Uh, yes, I'm...okay. Thank you, Chief Hansen." She hung up the phone and looked at Damien and Hodges who were both watching her intently.

"What gives?" Damien asked. She told them both everything Hansen had said.

"He should never have tried to bring her in alone," Damien said.

"My God, he worked with her for seven years. Who'd have thought he couldn't talk her into giving up? They had a good relationship and he knew her so well."

"You never completely know anyone," Hodges offered. "Of course, now we have to find her. I owe it to Cadence...And Richard Pieson," he added.

"I've gotta get ahold of Cooper," Beth said as she retrieved her cell phone from her pocket and dialed his number. It rang three times before Lewis picked up, sounding as if he had been drugged.

"Cooper," she said excitedly, "you're okay!"

His voice seemed to lose the drowsiness when he heard her voice.

"Beth, I'm damn lucky, or Lisa didn't shoot straight on purpose. I'm assuming Derrick Hansen got ahold of you and let you know what happened."

"Yes. I just hung up from him a few minutes ago."

"Did he also tell you that I was a damn fool for confronting her by myself?"

Beth didn't hesitate with her answer. "No, he didn't say a word, just wanted me to know about you."

"Well, I'm surprised by that, because he sure gave me an earful and more. I know it was a stupid thing to do and violated every law enforcement protocol imaginable, but Lisa and I've known and worked together for a long time and I wanted to give her the chance to explain to me why she did it and to surrender on her own. It would have looked better for her. Now…I don't know what she's going to do. She used some of her black belt stuff on me and I found out how strong she actually is. I always had wondered what she would be like in a fight and I hate to say it, but she's more than I can handle."

"Cooper, do you have any idea where she might go?" Beth asked.

"It's a long shot, but yeah. I've got one." Beth's eyes widened.

"Where?"

"I haven't told Hansen and Shanahan about the cabin, yet. Do you remember it."

"I do," she said in a quiet monotone.

"Beth, I want you and Damien to go there and I'll plan on meeting you within the hour. I still think we can bring her in without the police. No matter what she's done, I don't want to see Lisa killed. I'm afraid that's just what will happen if other law enforcement get involved." He paused, straining to hear her answer.

She looked toward Hodges, who had been able to hear both sides of the conversation. He was getting his coat, preparing to leave, Damien's Glock in his hand as he watched the two of them.

"I'm afraid, that's not possible now," was all Beth said and hung up the phone.

On the other end of the line, Lewis said, "Beth, Beth!" He shook the phone. "Damn cell phones disconnect you at the worst times."

"I wouldn't try anything Mr. George. Your gun is quite real, and I don't want to prove it. The three of us are going to the cabin I heard Sheriff Lewis mention, and search for Lisa."

"But…I'm not quite sure where it is," Beth protested.

"You will find it."

Beth and Damien gathered their coats as Hodges trained the gun on them. The three of them entered Damien's vehicle, with Hodges sitting in the back seat.

Chapter 22

The cabin was, literally, a cabin, although a very plush and comfortable one.   Pre-cut and numbered logs had been shipped to Dexter from a log cabin building business in northern Minnesota and assembled onsite by skilled congregants of Our Family Christian Church. It boasted three spacious bedrooms and four baths. A beautiful cathedral ceiling sheltered the rustic but glamorous living room/dining room areas. The kitchen was huge, containing every possible cooking appliance. Each bathroom even contained a bidet; very little expense had been spared when the church completed the "cabin."

It was set in a wooded area west and north of the little town of Dexter. Hodges kept his gun pointed toward the front seats as they approached the cabin from the southern point, fully aware the police might be in the area.

"I don't see any cars, police or otherwise," Damien said as his eyes scanned the area.

"Good, turn into the driveway and we will get out and look around," Hodges commanded. To their surprise, the driveway had been plowed and car tracks were evident, although no vehicles could be seen.

"We shouldn't be here, Gerald. The police could come any minute and we'll be arrested for harboring a fugitive…"

"And protecting a murderer," Damien added.

"If that happens, I'll tell them the truth, that I kidnapped you two and forced both of you to come here with me."

"Yeah, that makes me feel better," Damien uttered softly.

"What's that, Mr. George?"

"Nothing, just muttering to myself, Gerald, uh, I'm sorry, Mr. Hodges."

"You're learning, my boy." Damien cringed.

"I think it's strange the police haven't been here yet," Beth said as she looked around the cabin she had never actually been inside of. After the cult she had helped expose had been dissolved two years ago, she had twice toured the area surrounding the cabin with Cooper Lewis.

Hodges nudged them forward as he stood behind them with the gun. All three began walking toward the ornately carved front door tucked underneath the massive awning covering the porch.

As they walked up the two wooden steps and onto the porch, the floor boards didn't utter a creak or moan.

Beth stopped at the door, noticing the knob and lock had been tampered with. Could be anyone-probably kids, she thought. Beth glanced back at Hodges and Damien who had noticed the same thing and placed themselves on heightened alert. She slowly reached for the knob and turned it. The unlocked door opened easily as all eyes strained nervously to see what was inside the semi-darkened room.

They could have heard the proverbial pin drop in the silence that prevailed. Damien took the lead and cautiously stepped inside with Beth and Hodges following. He flipped on the light switch, but no light came on.

"Power must be turned off," Beth said, as she squinted and tried to focus on objects in the room.

Beth and Damien stood for several seconds, with Gerald Hodges securely behind them. They all pondered their next move.

When their eyes had fully adjusted to the low light conditions, dusty sheets covering the furniture were revealed. Damien swept a hand across a sheet covering the sofa and rubbed the accumulated dust between his fingers, letting the particles of dust scatter on the floor as his eyes continued searching the room for any sign of life.

"So this is where the people who made your childhood hell rested and recreated," Hodges said as he gazed around the living room. Beth said nothing, but kept her attention focused on discovering Lisa, if she was here at all.

"Let's split up and move around to the bedrooms," Damien suggested.

"No, we'll stay together. Safety in numbers you know," Hodges said, not wanting to let Damien or Beth out of his sight. They walked together through the living room, and then paused at the dining/kitchen area. Damien marveled out loud about the opulence of it all. Moving on, they checked out the first bedroom, a huge area with walk in closets and master bath. They did the same with the second bedroom. The third bedroom door was closed, sending red flags popping through all of their minds.

Approaching cautiously, Damien turned the knob and gave the door a gentle shove, swinging it mostly open. He entered first, with Beth close behind, followed by Hodges, who held the revolver securely in his right hand. All eyes stared directly ahead at a massive oak bedroom set consisting of king-sized bed, a vertical chest of drawers, a long, low chest, and two end tables flanking the bed. The master bathroom door was open, revealing the usual amenities.

All three were now standing within the room, glancing warily about.

"Put the gun down, Mr. Hodges," Lisa said as she emerged from behind the door.

"Oh for Christ's sakes, behind the door, really?" Damien exclaimed.

Hodges whirled around with his right arm holding the gun extended and ready to fire, but found himself in excruciating pain as Lisa brought her nightstick down hard on his wrist, sending the revolver skittering across the hardwood floor. Lisa retrieved it quickly before Beth or Damien could respond.

Hodges writhed in pain as no one moved to help him.

"How does it feel to be on the receiving end of a nightstick, Mr. Hodges?" Lisa asked sarcastically. Hodges said nothing, but held his wrist and grimaced.

"Lisa, the police may be here soon. Let us help you," Beth pleaded.

"I'm pretty sure Cooper hasn't told anyone else about this place, so I don't expect them to be coming within the next hour at least," Lisa responded. "And I don't know how you're going to help me now. Cooper knows everything, meaning the rest of the team will know it soon. I know he wanted to talk me into giving myself up and make sure that I wasn't harmed by the police. He was also worried about my emotional state."

"Yes, that's exactly what he didn't want, Lisa. That's why he told us about this place and the possibility you may have come here to, to, just think."

"Yes, think. Think about what I did, my life, or lack of…Did he tell you anything about why I killed Pieson and Claude?"

"No," Lisa said.

"Beth, you, more than anyone here, should be able to understand why I did it. You were abused as a child. You lived a horrible life into your young adulthood. Terrible people exist in this world and you have first-hand knowledge of that. My childhood wasn't that much different from yours. My father abused my mom and me. He'd get drunk, hit, kick, slap, and yell at us."

"So you killed Claude and Cadence because of your father?" Damien asked.

"In a way I did… yes. I grew up without the love of a father, a real man who would hold me on his lap, treat me like his little girl, play games with me… He didn't even love my mother, much less, me."

"It all makes sense to me," Hodges managed to say through his grimaces.

"Shut up, you pervert," Lisa said evenly, as she looked directly at him. "You are one of those people who doesn't deserve to live. I relished the thought of using what you did to cover up my own crime. You fit in so perfectly with your penchant for dressing up. I knew I would be recorded by the security cameras in Claude's apartment house. It wouldn't have taken much for everyone to believe that I was you. My face was hidden and obviously, I was in women's clothing. It was just like your MO, right Hodges?" She didn't bother to wait for an answer, but continued talking. Her head drooped a little, and then she said, "But Cooper figured it out. I guess he recognized the way I walked in the security tape. Wonder of wonders, a man who actually noticed me over the years and paid attention to me."

"So you shot the only man who paid quality attention to you. That's how you repaid him, huh?" It was more of a statement that Damien uttered, than a question.

"I didn't mean to shoot Cooper. It was an accident," Lisa said remorsefully.

"Lisa, I still don't get why you killed Cadence and Peltier," Beth confessed.

"Why don't you understand, Beth? It's so simple. Love, or rather, the lack of it."

"You loved Peltier?"

"No…but I wished I had. I knew he didn't love me. He started out as a convenience, like a nice pair of slippers that you can't get rid of no matter how tattered or worn out they become. He paid attention to me and we had sex, lots of it, but that's all it ever was to him, and it turns out, me. When Cadence began seeing him, all I could think of was why her, and not me. He didn't even want to see me anymore, never answered my telephone calls or responded to notes I left on his apartment door."

"So you were jealous," Beth said.

"I suppose I was, and I became so…so…angry about it. I wanted him to love me, not her. I just needed someone to pay attention to me, to love me! There was no chance of it ever happening, but I needed that. I don't know, it seems so weird to me now."

"You killed the woman I loved," Hodges said unemotionally.

"You think she cared about you, Hodges? She didn't even know you existed. You were lying to yourself if you ever thought so."

Hodges said pathetically, "I was going to tell her what I had done to make her happy, to further her career. Maybe then...she would have felt something for me."

"More drivel from a pervert, slash, idiot." Lisa drew an imaginary, diagonal line in the air. "Hodges, you are a sick man who deserves to be in jail or dead. Lucky for all of us that will happen soon."

"Spoken like a real human being," Damien said disgustedly.

"Listen Junior, as the old guys called you, it's all relative. I grew up with an abusive, alcoholic father and an enabler of a mother. She let herself...me, be used by that disgusting human being who called himself my father. Life is full of despicable individuals who look like human beings, but fail the test on every accepted measure of what's right and good. I became a cop so that I could help right the wrongs and put creeps like Hodges... or my father, away forever."

"Lisa, I suffered as much as anyone. You don't have to let people continue to control your life when they're not even around anymore. That's what you've done. You've let your father dictate how you view everyone and you're still looking at people through the prism he gave you. It doesn't have to be that way."

Lisa clapped slowly, being careful not to drop the Glock. "Thank you Doctor Elizabeth Reddy, amateur psychiatrist."

Giving up, Beth asked, "So what now, Lisa? Where do we go from here?"

"A few things have been floating through my mind. One of which is this. You need to tie Hodges up." She produced quarter inch diameter rope from her jacket pocket and tossed it to Beth. When Beth was finished, Lisa produced another piece of rope and tossed it to Beth. "Now tie up Junior." Beth did as she was instructed and then Lisa inspected the job. The rope was loosely wound around Damien's wrists. "Nice try, Beth. I guess I would have done the same." She took out a pair of handcuffs and flipped them to Beth. "Use these." Beth clamped them to Damien's wrists, which were already tied behind his back. "Now wrap this around his ankles and tie it to the cuffs." She threw another short piece of rope at Beth, who did what Lisa wanted her to do.

After finishing the task, Beth stood up and asked, "Now what?"

"Now you and I are going to take a walk out to the woods and settle this."

A confused look appeared on Beth's face. "What do you mean? Settle what?"

"Let's go." She pointed the revolver at Beth and motioned her to the door. Damien started yelling for them to stop. "Wait, one more thing." Lisa walked over to Damien, withdrew duct tape out of her pocket and slapped it over his mouth, muting his cries. "I've found that the uses of duct tape are endless. Never leave home without it." She looked over at Hodges.

"No need for that on me," he said. "You won't hear a peep." Lisa looked at him and then ripped off a strip and plastered it over his mouth. "I think we're ready now," she said.

A cold gust of wind smacked Beth in the face when she opened the back door and walked out onto a snow-covered patio, followed by Lisa.

"There," Lisa pointed to the little woods thirty yards to the north of the cabin. Beth truly felt she was heading for an execution, but she couldn't imagine why. They entered the woods and walked until they came to a clearing that resembled a mini arena.

"Turn around, Beth."

"So you want me to see it coming when you empty your gun into me?"

Lisa appeared dumbfounded by the question.

"I don't want to kill you, Beth!"

"Then, why? Why are we out here now, away from the others?"

"I thought we needed privacy for what we were going to do," she said as she took off her jacket and wrapped the gun into it, placing it twenty feet away. She then walked back towards Beth, who was looking more confused than ever. The temperature hovered around twenty-eight degrees, but there was no wind and the sun shown brilliantly upon them, making the air feel much warmer.

"You should remove your jacket, Beth. You'll move more freely when you do." Beth began to get the picture and took off her coat.

"Before we begin. We are doing this because…?" The intonation of Beth's voice rose when she didn't finish the question, begging Lisa to answer.

"I'm a competitive person, Beth, and I've watched you work out. You are good, but I think I'm better. We're doing this…just because I wanted to."

Beth paused with her mouth open and head tilted like a confused cocker spaniel, before saying something. "I never knew you were so strange, Lisa. And I don't say that to demean you. I'm just weirded out by this entire scenario, I guess." Slightly hunched over, they circled each other, gauging the other's posture and demeanor.

"One more thing," Beth began. "You do know that Cooper will be here soon, don't you?"

Lisa continued looking for an opening as she responded, "I figured he would be, so let's get the show rolling." Making a move like a wrestler, Lisa propelled her body low and straight ahead, aiming for Beth's legs. Beth sprawled her legs behind her as she collapsed her body on top of Lisa's back while wrapping her arms around her chest.

Krav Maga had taught Beth how to survive using every brutal method a person could ever think of. Her willingness to use those methods was being put to the test now. Lisa had already said she didn't want to kill her. This was a fight, not to the death, but in Lisa's weird mind, to see who was better, whatever that meant.

Beth tried holding onto Lisa, but she felt that it surely must feel like this to ride a bucking steer, for Lisa was trying every type of move imaginable to free herself of Beth's grip. Finally she couldn't hold on any longer, released her grip and jumped backwards to be immediately free of any counterattack that might…check that, would come.

"Nice job, Beth, you handled that very smoothly. Now let's see what happens when I…" Lisa swept a boot at her head, barely missing because of Beth's quick reflexes. Then a series of leg sweeps from Lisa backed Beth against the tree line.

"Come on, Beth. You're just playing defense here. Put yourself in attack mode for a while. Come on, let's see what you've got." Trying to look at this as a match in the gym, Beth unleashed a flurry of punches and leg sweeps of her own, backing Lisa up and nearly knocking her down. Ignoring her earlier confusion about why they were doing this, Beth was reflexively fighting now. Lisa had said she didn't want to kill her, so this was just a contest. She could handle that. It was a contest Beth thought she could win, although she knew Lisa felt the same about her chances. They went back and forth, feinting, lunging, kicking, and punching. Lisa sported a bloody nose now and Beth's ribs burned from two sharp kicks a minute earlier.

They continued to go at each other, layering blow upon blow as they tired, neither one giving in to the other. And then Lisa was able to knock Beth down with a smothering flurry of punches to the head and upper body. Beth lay on her back in the snow, breathless.

Lisa stood over her beaten foe. "You see," she said between pants. "I knew I was better than you." The only sounds they could hear in those moments were the pants coming from their bloodied mouths until Gerald Hodges appeared at the edge of the snow covered arena. Beth noticed him first as he approached, and began to scramble to her feet.

"You're ready for more, huh Beth? Well, okay, let's have at it," Lisa said as she backed up a little.

"Gerald, no, you can't." Lisa wheeled around to see Hodges pointing Damien's Glock at her. He didn't wait for her to say anything, but simply shot her in the head, killing her before she collapsed in the snow. Beth screamed and clambered over the snow to

Lisa, knowing there was nothing she could do to save her, but reflexes again had taken over. Hodges stood, holding the gun, looking as empty as any man possibly could. The sun glistened off his forehead as tears became tiny rivulets and dribbled down his cheeks.

"That was for Cadence," he said quietly. And then he turned the revolver towards Beth. "Do not attempt to stop me, Ms. Reddy, because, if I have to, I will disable you. Your friend, Mr. George, is still in the house."

"You didn't…"

"Kill him? No need, he's incapacitated. Besides, I would not take a loved one from you. He is quite uncomfortable, but alive. You should go to him now."

Beth scrambled to her feet and ran towards the cabin, stopping to turn back and yell to Hodges. "Gerald, please, give yourself up. Sheriff Lewis will be here soon and we'll do everything we can to put you in a good hospital…please, for me."

He looked tired and old as his shoulders slumped toward the snow and thin wisps of white hair flopped over his forehead. He only said, "Go," and then began walking away. She ran to the cabin and found Damien trying to squirm out of the handcuffs while his muffled cries reflected back on himself.

He screamed when she ripped the duct tape from his mouth. "Beth, Beth, I thought you'd been shot. He left here and I heard the shot and I, I…" He seemed out of breath after having talked so fast. "I didn't want anything to happen to you." He abruptly stopped speaking and stared at her for a moment. "What happened, where are Lisa and Hodges?"

"Lisa is dead. Hodges shot her. How did he get out of here?"

"I really don't know," he said, while shaking his head. "The guy is like a magician. I heard him moving around and a little later he was up and running out of here. Where is he now? Is he out there? Is he going to turn himself in?" He looked at her searchingly, trying to read her masked expression.

"I don't know. He told me to go here and be with you."

"Wha...What? You've gotta get me out of this before he comes back." He struggled desperately against the handcuffs and rope. Beth undid the rope and he managed to contort his arms and legs enough to bring his cuffed hands to the front.

"We should stay here until Cooper arrives," Beth said as she hugged him close.

Panting, preoccupied with Hodges, and sore from the struggle of trying to escape his bonds, Damien suddenly realized how beat up Beth was. He looked at her.

"What happened between you and Lisa out there?"

Beth shook her head and shrugged her shoulders before she said, "Lisa wanted to fight to find out who was better."

He looked at her with confused, unbelieving eyes. "She wanted to fight you? That's what it was all about out there?"

"I think she was going to give up, but first, she had this crazy, weird need to find out who the better fighter was. I really think she had decided to give herself up to Cooper when he came, but since we were here, she had to satisfy her curiosity." He looked at her again, not really believing her explanation, but now it was his turn to shrug his shoulders and shake his head.

She helped him to his feet and they stood still for a moment, not knowing what to do or where to go. Finally, Beth said, "My phone. Where is it?" They searched around the room with no luck. "It must be outside in my jacket. I took it off when Lisa and I fought." They moved toward the northern window in the kitchen and looked out into the yard, searching for signs of Hodges. When they saw none, Damien said he would chance the walk out to where she and Lisa had battled.

Beth said, "No Damien, Hodges would be more likely to leave me alone than you. I'll go." He touched her shoulder and told her to be careful. They kissed, and then she was out the back door, sprinting toward the arena. When she hit the edge of the woods she slowed down and began walking at a normal pace. She stopped at the arena where Lisa lay dead. No sign of Hodges appeared anywhere.

Her jacket lay on the far edge of the little clearing. When she reached it, she combed the pockets for her phone. It wasn't there. Hodges must have taken it or buried it in the snow somewhere. She saw tracks moving north and east toward I-90. Quickly, she turned around and ran back to the cabin where Damien met her at the back door.

"The phone wasn't there and neither was Hodges. I saw tracks heading north and to the interstate."

"We have no way of contacting anyone from here and Hodges is getting away. We could walk into Dexter and contact Cooper and the others. It isn't far, maybe half a mile or so," Damien said.

Beth agreed. "Okay, I'll grab my coat and we can start walking." She ran back to the clearing and picked up her coat. When she arrived back at the cabin she could hear Cooper's voice. Thank God, she said to herself.

They were standing just inside the doorway of the cabin. Cooper was ridding Damien of the handcuffs while Damien was recounting in rapid detail some of what had occurred in the last few minutes. Cooper seemed to be wincing in pain as he bent down to remove the cuffs.

"Cooper, I sure wish you had arrived here fifteen minutes earlier," Beth said breathlessly as she finished her run to the cabin.

"Yeah, well I wish I had been here earlier too. Where's Lisa?"

"I haven't had time to tell him," Damien said apologetically.

"Tell me what? What?" Cooper said almost hysterically.

"She's dead. Hodges killed her."

"What the hell, whaddaya mean? Hodges was here? How? Why?" Cooper appeared dumbfounded as his look pressed them for the details.

When they finished the story of how Hodges had come to be at the cabin, Cooper fell silent for a minute, wanting desperately to digest and accept everything they had told him. Finally, Lewis took out his cell phone and called Derrick Hansen, informing him of the situation. After he hung up, he said Lisa's name aloud in a sad, painful voice. He then walked out of the cabin to where she lay.

Twenty minutes later, several squad cars pulled up in front of the cabin and armed officers spread out to comb the area for Hodges. Units had also been sent to the interstate area and nearby homes in their search of him.

A day and a half later, they still hadn't found Gerald Hodges and any leads that came in turned out to be useless. The man had vanished.

Hodges watched Beth run to the cabin, turned and walked to her coat. He retrieved her cell phone and began walking north and east out of the clearing. After walking a quarter of a mile, Hodges stopped and dropped to his knees. A sudden meltdown of emotions collided within his brain, sending him into a downward spiral of despair.

He withdrew the Glock from his pocket, shakily placed the nozzle of the gun to his right temple, closed his eyes and lightly squeezed the trigger. His mind raced. What was left for him now? His neurons and synapses fired and snapped, sending conflicting signals across the surface of his brain. A trembling hand held the revolver closer to his head and the finger pressing against the trigger contracted a millimeter farther.

Everything seemed to be crashing around him and he felt as if he were falling into a deep cavern, while waving his hands and shouts of "Help me!" flowed from his mouth. And then, the pace of his fall slowed and he was floating. His arms stopped waving and peacefulness enveloped him. The firing neurons cooled and he slowly began to realize his purpose in life. He rose from his knees and began walking again.

After traveling a hundred yards, he dialed a number, spoke for only a minute and then tossed the phone into the snow. Three hundred yards later he emerged onto a lonely county road where the rented SUV was waiting. The rear passenger door swung open, beckoning him inside. He did not disappoint the occupant, racing as fast as his fifty-five year old legs would allow him.

Five days later, Carin Loggerton, Celia Orth and Beth Reddy met for lunch at Kenny's Oak Grill in Austin. The topic of conversation hovered around the book club murders, Gerald Hodges, and Lisa Dolcheski. The latest mystery, of course, was what had become of Gerald Hodges and how he escaped the extensive dragnet that had been deployed to capture him. Ideas were flung out by the group like they were tossing peanuts and candy to the kids at a Fourth of July parade. The fact of the matter was, however, that all of them seemed too fantastic to be real.

None of the group had suspected Lisa Dolcheski of ever having been involved in the murders or that her life had been as tortured as she had described to Beth. As for Hodges, little or no sympathy for him emanated from any of the gathered souls, except for Beth, who continued to exude a strange mixture of empathy and outrage when she spoke of him.

They talked of how the police had followed his tracks to a county road, where they assumed he had commandeered a passing auto and forced the driver to take him somewhere. The assumption proved to be troubling because no one ever reported such an incident and the police were hard pressed to come up with an alternative, other than it had been a prearranged meeting.

Beth had recalled how they had left him alone in their house while she and Damien had gone to Rose Creek to view the security tapes and how he could have called someone then. Her phone records had not been checked as of yet nor had her cell phone been recovered. If a call had been made it had not been discovered, but she thought it was only a matter of time.

Epilogue

Lucille Amberworth walked down the stairs of the Boeing 737 and set foot on Australian soil for the first time in months. The temperature was 93 degrees Fahrenheit and waves of heat swamped her as she began walking the tarmac toward a small crowd of people gathered behind a fence. She smiled when she heard shouts of "Grandma, Grandma." The words of her grandchildren warmed her far more than the heat being delivered on that late day in January.

Her pace, along with the chants of joy, quickened as she neared the children. This was going to be the best welcome back celebration she had ever had. And then, more shouts came. "Uncle Gerry, Uncle Gerry, we love you." Lucille turned to Gerald Hodges as he slung his carry-on bag over his shoulder, and smiled at the man she loved. He took her hands in his, and smiled back.

About the Author

Jeffrey Jan (J.J.) Ollman is a retired Speech/Language Pathologist who began writing novels in 2009. He lives with his wife, Cindy, in southeastern Minnesota and enjoys writing, traveling, reading, hiking, and an occasional glass of wine or two with friends.

His next novel, Brothers, will be released in April of 2015.

Made in the USA
Monee, IL
20 November 2022

18218588R00125